MATT CHISHOLM, 1919—

GUN LUST

Complete and Unabridged

LINFORD
Leicester

A-1

First published in Great Britain in 1968 by
Panther Books Limited,
London

First Linford Edition
published March 1987

British Library CIP Data

Chisholm, Matt
  Gun lust.—Large print ed.—
Linford western library
Rn: Peter Watts   I. Title
823'.914[F]   PR6073.A8/

  ISBN 0-7089-6349-8

Published by
F. A. Thorpe (Publishing) Ltd.
Anstey, Leicestershire

Set by Rowland Phototypesetting Ltd.
Bury St. Edmunds, Suffolk
Printed and bound in Great Britain by
T. J. Press (Padstow) Ltd., Padstow, Cornwall

1

THEY stood and stared at the dried up waterhole and they knew that death had stalked nearer.

Arch turned and looked at the line of wagons, at the mules with their drooping heads, wondering how much longer they could last.

Mel Dawford said: "You know what? If'n we don't find water tomorrow, we're finished."

Mel wasn't the kind of man to panic, but he knew this country. He had come on this trip with his eyes wide open. He had done the wagon run to Crewsville a couple of hundred times. He knew every inch of the ground. He knew that if there wasn't water here, there wouldn't be water at the next stop. It was the wrong time of the year for the trip. They had both known that before they started. More than that—it was the wrong year.

This was the year of the Apache. This was the year in which something like seven thousand soldiers hunted no more than thirty-five Apache who had broken from the reservation

1

under Juanito. Those who knew or claimed to know said that among the band there were no more than twenty fighting men. The rest were women and kids. But they had hogtied several counties and had tied up an army, crossing and recrossing the Mexican Border at will, harrying the settlers till whole counties were deserted by settlers, killing and burning with a destructiveness that bordered on the insane.

Arch had fought Indians in the Panhandle, in Kansas and Montana, but he had never met anything like the utter ferocity of the Apache. And God knew that the Cheyenne and the Sioux were impressive enough. The Apache didn't have the numbers, but they possessed something that took the place of numbers. It was a will to destroy and to hate. Some men thought of them as animals to be shot on sight, but no animal possessed the ferocious cunning that they exhibited in their war to the death against the whiteman.

Juanito had not spoken much with whitemen, but always in his rare meetings with them, he had impressed them with the fact that he believed that he had right on his side. This was his land. The whiteman had no right here. Therefore the whiteman must be held responsible for anything that happened to white people who came into it.

Arch Kelso, burned out and broke, his cattle slaughtered by the Indians, had taken this desperate gamble to recoup his fortunes. Crewsville, gold-mining and cattle country center, was stuffed tight with gold and was low on food and supplies. If you wanted the gold, the answer was simple—take supplies to Crewsville. Arch had turned naturally to Mel Dawford. Mel knew the country and Arch knew Mel. All they had needed was wagons, supplies and men.

The answer to that was Tucson to the southwest. Tucson had suffered from Indian incursions to the surrounding countryside, but had not felt the squeeze as Crewsville had. Supplies were still plentiful there. They were easy to find. But the money to buy them and the men to drive the wagons had not been. The men in Tucson had gathered there in the face of Apache terror, few wanted to risk the Indians again.

It took a week to find the money; two to find the men. Arch and Mel ended up with six wagons, their teams and two men per wagon. For safety's sake, they had taken along a dozen spare mules. They had made one mistake. They were in the enterprise for profit and they hadn't sacrificed supplies for water and they should have done. Now they were paying. Mel, for once, had been wrong. He had reckoned on enough water to get them to Crewsville and he had been wrong.

He stood now, staring at the dried-up water-hole and looking like a man who had made the mistake of his life. In his hands he had not only held the futures of himself and Arch Kelso, but the lives of fourteen men. He had gambled and almost lost. All the men there thought he had lost. But Mel had one hope left. He knew the country.

"We can't go on," he said. "We can't turn back."

Kelso said: "Hunt's Tank is only a day from here. The mules'll hold up till there."

Mel shook his head.

"There'll be none there. That's the way our luck's goin'."

"I'll ride on an' take a look," Arch said.

"An' lose your hair."

"You don't know there's Indians around."

"You don't know there ain't."

Arch looked toward the men lying in the shade of the wagons, waiting for Mel to come

4

to his decision. They all trusted him. Fear had not touched them yet. It would not be long before it did.

Arch said: "Somebody has to do somethin' an' quick."

Mel said: "Anybody's goin' to be a hero, it's me. I owe."

Arch looked at his partner angrily.

"You don't owe a damn thing. We all knew we took a gamble."

Mel looked toward the hills. His eyes fell on the divide. Beyond there, there was water. He was sure of that. But how to get it down here to the men and mules. Arch saw where he was looking.

"There's water up there," he said.

Mel nodded. He filled his pipe and started puffing.

"It'd take a wagon," he said. "We need water a-plenty."

"Sure," Arch said, "I'll go."

They argued about that. They got heated. They shouted a little and the drowsing men raised their heads to listen. The nearby mules stirred. Finally, Mel said: "If you insist on bein' a damn fool, we'll both go. Charlie Garth can take charge here." Arch Kelso accepted that.

5

The danger of the hills touched him. They discussed whether the wagon-train should be left here and decided that it was best. The mules were played out. The ground was pretty open here and the men with the wagon had a fair chance of spotting Indians, or as much chance as anybody could have of spotting Apache when they didn't want to be spotted.

Then, having made their decision, doubt set in. The wagons were to be left in the open where they could be seen for miles around. The supplies would be like honey to bees. Everything that the Indian renegades needed was there for the taking. Arch voiced his doubts.

Mel knocked out his pipe and said: "I know. I got the same feelin'. But what other chance do we have? Tell me that."

So they walked along the line of wagons and gathered the men together. They came, unshaven and unwashed, looking exactly what they were, men honed down by heat and thirst. They were down to a canteen of water a day in a climate which tempted a man to drink twenty times that amount. But they were still a unit, men with a common danger and a common need. Charlie Garth, a little sawn-off whip of a man who had fought Indians for the last twenty years, managed a joke that set them all chuckling. He was thin, so thin that he didn't seem to sweat a drop. The desert land had claimed him long ago. He knew the trail to Tucson as well as Mel did. He knew Apaches. He had wit, cunning and guts. There wasn't much more a man needed in a situation like this.

Mel hunkered down and the others followed suit, all except young Joe Debson and he stood on a wagon seat and kept his sharp young eyes on the country, looking for telltale wisps of dust.

Mel hitched his long Colt's gun onto his right buttock and said: "I don't have to tell you, boys, that we're in a fix. It's my fault. I should have known. To even things up Arch an' me'll raise your share in the stake. By the time we're done, you'll have earned it. There's a tank a day's ride from here, but we can't gamble on that. I know an eye over the saddle yonder. I daresay Charlie knows it." Garth nodded. "Me an' Arch'll take a wagon an' bring water back here. Charlie'll take charge here. Laager the wagons, set a strong watch and look out for dust. If you don't see no dust, Juanito's likely there. Or that's the way you should think. Charlie knows that. Me an' Arch'll be gone two

7

days, maybe three. You got to hold out that time."

Charlie Garth tried to spit and couldn't find enough saliva for the job.

"We'll do it," he said. "Eh, boys?"

They grunted their assent.

Ben Goodall asked: "Can two men make it, if you run into trouble, Mel?"

Charlie cut in with: "I don't reckon."

Arch said: "This is our deal. We made the mistake. It's up to us to make it good."

Ben said: "You won't make it good if you're dead."

"I go along with that," Charlie said.

"So I vote I go along too," Ben offered.

The men murmured their agreement.

Charlie Garth said: "You gotta have at least three, Mel. Three's a risk, God knows."

Mel nodded. "All right," he said. "Thanks, Ben." He stood up and Arch told the men to laager the wagons. The men got on the move at once, circling the vehicles with the teams inside the circle and then unhitching the teams. Arch ordered one wagon left outside the circle and a fresh team to be hitched to it. It was hot sweating work under the broiling sun. When it was done, men hefted the water containers and all the empty canteens they could find and put them into the wagon. Then Mel, Arch and Ben picked their saddle horses. Inside an hour, they were ready to move out. Charlie and the rest of the men gathered around to shake them by the hand and wish them luck. Arch climbed aboard the wagon, while Mel and Ben stepped into the saddle. There was three hours of daylight left to them as they pulled slowly away. Arch lined up the wagon for the saddle in the hills and knew that probably he could hold it to that course till they hit the foothills. Then Mel would be the guide. Then they would be in country where Indians could breathe down their necks without being sighted. Arch felt a little sick at the thought and wondered if his two companions felt the same. It was like riding to your own funeral.

They reached the first ridge, looked back at the wagons and the men watching them out of sight and went on. There was no sound but the plodding hoofs of the mules and the creak of the wagon. Now and then a mule snorted. Mel smoked his pipe as he rode off to one side of the wagon. He looked like a sack of hay tied in the middle, an untidy red-faced man who should, by all appearances, have been an eastern

9

farmer. He looked stolid, unimaginative, bucolic and slow. His appearance was deceptive. Arch knew. He had seen him fight with fist, knife and gun.

Off to the other side, rode Ben Goodall, one-time cattleman, never very successful, but a good man to side you in a fight. He liked to laugh and a smile came easily to his long sunburned face out of which a pair of cold pale eyes stared. He had brush-popped in south-west Texas, driven a stage in Kansas, gold-mined in California and run a saloon in Tombstone. Once he had drifted onto the wrong side of the law, then made that failing good by serving a term as a town marshal somewhere up in Montana. To Arch's knowledge, he had killed two men in what might be considered by the squeamish as fair fight. He had lost a wife and two children the year before in an Apache raid and had never been quite the same since. That same raid had not only finished him emotionally, but financially as well. Every cent he had in the world had been invested in cattle. Nobody need doubt his hatred of Apaches. Nor need anybody doubt that, if a fight with the Indians were offered, he would take it up.

Arch reckoned he was in good company. And

he reckoned before this trip was done he was going to need it.

He sat on the swaying and jerking wagon seat, shifting his eyes from the mules and up to the threatening hills that marched slowly closer. At his side was the latest model of the Winchester repeater, one investment that Mel had insisted on. How right he had been would be proved before long.

But, Arch thought, *we don't know that Juanito's within a hundred miles of here*.

The thought didn't give him any confidence. Juanito always knew when anything moved across the face of what he regarded as his domain. Juanito was up there all right, maybe right on the saddle itself, where ambush was easy and a half-dozen determined men could hold up an army.

Maybe, Arch thought, *it's better to stay alive than to make your stake*. But the thought came too late. He was in this thing right up to his neck.

2

HOW news ever filtered across the Apache-infested desert nobody could say, but filter it did. Or maybe it was no more than rumor. Whatever it was, men in Crewsville accepted it as the gospel truth. A man with a scar down one side of his face, and who wore a gun at his waist even in town, heard a certain piece of news while taking his first drink of the day around noon in the *Golden Lady*. He was a down-at-heel, kind of a cast-off-looking individual who might have been mistaken by a pilgrim as a cowhand, but to anybody who had seen the elephant he was plainly a hardcase, shy of work and dedicated to the belief that the world owed him a living. He looked too as if, when the world did not offer him a living, he would take it at the point of a gun.

He would have liked another drink, for he had the money in his pocket for a change, but when he heard the news that two men near him claimed had come in from Tucson, some instinct told him that the sooner Doc Dooley heard it the better. There would be the price of several drinks in it possibly and maybe more. So he downed the remains of his drink and walked out of the saloon like a man who hates to use his legs except to wrap them around the barrel of a horse.

He knew where to find Doc this time of the day. He would be sitting on the edge of his bed, it now being around noon, lighting a smoke and taking his first drink. Only after this ceremony had been gone through would Doc anywhere near resemble a human being. Some were unkind enough to say that he never did.

The man with the scarred face walked down Main, turned into Donovan, angled across it and came to a house with what had once been a white picket fence around it. The house had once been the envy of the town, but that was before Doc had won it from the former owner at poker. Now it looked shabby and forlorn. Doc might like to dress flashily, but he didn't worry too much about houses.

The door was open, as was to be expected, because Doc with all his funny ways, liked to keep open house and, in spite of his frequent moroseness, liked the company of his fellow men, however much he might despise them. Or even because he liked to despise them.

In the empty hallway, the man with the scar stopped and called: "Anybody to home."

The inarticulate sound of a human voice came from above and the man accepted that as an invitation to come on up. He tramped up the stairs and walked into the first room he came to above. As he expected, Doc sat on the edge of the bed with a cigar between his rubber lips and a large glass of whiskey in one hand. He was dressed in ragged and very unclean long-johns. They were unbuttoned at the chest and revealed tangled gray hairs. Doc was unshaven and his hair was tussled. He looked at the man with the scar out of small red-rimmed eyes that blinked as though focusing were one hell of a chore this time of the day. Only after dark did Doc appear to come fully awake.

He was a man of medium height in his middle forties and he looked physically soft and mentally hard. He looked slow and lethargic. He looked a mite stupid, as though he had drunk away years back the few brains that God had given him. The man with the scar knew that this wasn't so. Doc was cunning, tough in every way known to man and could, when he

14

so desired, move as quick as the fastest man alive. He could out-ride, out-fight, out-drink and out-whore most men half his age. And was proud of it.

He looked at the man with the scar as if he were something a carrion crow wouldn't touch.

"Howdy, Doc."

"Howdy, Ringus."

Doc poured himself another drink after he had downed the one in his hand and the man with the scar didn't miss a move. He licked his lips.

"I could sure use a drink, Doc."

Doc nodded.

"I'd take a bet on it."

Ringus shifted his feet.

"I could earn one and maybe more."

Doc downed the second drink and watched Ringus' face with morose joy. Doc sighed with pleasure, scratched himself, heaved himself to his feet and staggered, as though sleep still half-possessed him, to a basin of dirty water that stood on a table in a corner of the room. With the cigar still smoking in his mouth, he started to soap his face with a wellworn brush. He hummed tunelessly as he did so. Then, while he stropped his cut-throat razor, he said: "You're bustin' to talk, man, so talk."

Ringus said: "I heard it in the *Golden Lady*. Man swore it was true bill."

"Which means it's another rumor."

"This is gospel, Doc."

"Go ahead."

Doc finished stropping and started to scrape the soap from his face, pulling weird contortions that seemed to fascinate Ringus who went on: "News from Tucson."

Doc stopped scraping and stared malignly at Ringus.

"How in hell can news come from Tucson, man? There ain't been a livin' soul come this way from Tucson in a half-year."

"You know how it is, Doc."

"I know how it is. Goddam rumors. All lies." He started scraping again and told Ringus: "Go ahead."

"Mel Dawford and Arch Kelso have started a wagon-train of supplies this way. Jesus, if they reached here with a train, they could clean up. Think of all that money, Doc. This here place is a-bustin' with gold, there ain't a damn thing to eat and even water's fetchin' a price."

Ringus stood watching while Doc finished his

shave, didn't notice the fact that Doc never wiped the soap off with water and failed to wash, but dry-wiped where he had shaved and at once started to pull on his clothes. This consisted of a fine lawn shirt, white as snow, a fine store suit of dark cloth which showed off the shirt and the crimson silk vest to perfection. Doc tied a thin neck-tie around his throat and heaved on a pair of exquisite hand-tooled boots and was ready for the world.

"You've earned a drink," he said, poured one for himself and for Ringus and handed the other a glass. Ringus hurled it down his throat and gasped with happiness. When he had regained his breath, he said: "I been thinkin'."

Doc looked at him in surprise.

"Don't spoil it," he said.

"No, listen," Ringus insisted. "The wagons come into a place like this full of supplies and them two sell 'em at whatever fancy prices they want. It's a seller's market. They got it made. They're goin' to have a hell of a lot of money on 'em when they're finished. You with me?"

Doc chuckled and the sound startled Ringus.

"You really have been thinkin', Ringus." He took Ringus' glass and poured him another drink.

17

"But that ain't all."

Doc raised his bushy eyebrows.

"You mean you thought more'n that?"

"Listen. Nobody brings wagons into Crewsville full and takes 'em back to Tucson empty."

Doc said: "If they come through Apache country and got through alive, they'd be damn foolish to take 'em back at all."

Ringus looked eager. "You ain't thinkin' so good, Doc. Maybe it's too early for you yet."

"You mean you've got another thought. Easy now, Ringus, you'll do yourself a mischief."

"Quit joshin' me, Doc. Dawford an' Kelso're trusted men. You know that. Nobody's been able to get gold out of this place ever since Juanito went on the warpath. If them two can get here alive, the diggers're goin' to reckon they can get back alive."

Doc nodded.

"You know, for once, Ringus, you're makin' some sort of sense. Dawford and Kelso take out gold." He drifted away then into his thoughts. After a while, he suddenly came back to the present and said: "If your yarn's true an' they do come, then there'll be work for you, boy."

"Do I get another drink, Doc, or somethin'?"

Doc fished in his pocket and spun Ringus a golden eagle. Ringus caught it deftly.

Doc said: "You talk about this an' you'll get nothin' more. Or maybe you'll get somethin' that ain't too welcome. Hear? So keep your mouth buttoned up an' there can be profit in this for both of us."

"Sure, Doc. You know me."

"Yeah, I know you. Now get outa here an' stay sober. Hear anythin', bring it to me."

Ringus shuffled his feet, tried a grin of loyalty and understanding that Doc ignored and got out of there.

Doc walked out of the room, along the landing and entered a room at the rear of the house. Here was a man snoring in bed. Doc whipped the bed-clothes off him and prodded him with a hard forefinger. The man groaned and opened his eyes. Doc said: "Get up."

Without a word, the man got off the bed and stood in front of Doc. Even in his long-johns and bare feet, still groggy from sleep, he showed himself to be a magnificent looking man. Well over six feet tall, broad in the shoulder and narrow in the hips, a mane of fair hair and a long fair mustache. Eyes of icy blue.

"Witt, where're your brothers?" Doc demanded.

"How should I know?"

"Don't give me no sass. Go find 'em an' bring 'em here."

"I ain't through sleepin'."

"Get some clothes on and get the boys. Right now."

The big man blinked, pulling himself together. He knew when Doc meant business. He started pulling his clothes on, dully ticking off the places where his three brothers might be. Rod over at the saloon maybe; Dirk at home with his loving wife; Stet in the whorehouse most likely.

Doc walked out of the room and went downstairs. He went into the kitchen. Rosa, the Mexican girl that Doc and some of the boys shared, was making coffee. It smelled good. Doc pinched her right buttock and she gave him a friendly smile.

"Smells good," Doc said.

He sat down at the table, drinking coffee and listened to the sound of Witt going out of the house. The coffee was good. He enjoyed it and the thoughts that built on the rumor that Ringus had brought him. If it was true, this

20

could be the biggest chance of his life. There was only one snag. Dawford and Kelso could look out for themselves.

3

THEY spent the night on the edge of the
foothills amid a wild landscape that could
have been the surface of the moon that
shone down coldly on them, making the night
bright enough for a man to imagine that he
could see stealthy movement, but never enough
for him to be sure. One watched, rifle in hands,
while two slept. In the hills above, a lobo
mourned life in doleful song. There was little
or no grass for the mules and no water to speak
of. They tied them to the wagon, rinsed their
mouths with a little water and tried in vain to
make them eat corn.

The three men spent an uneasy night, twice
with the guard giving a false alarm. The two
awoken men didn't grumble. They would rather
have a jumpy guard now than a sleeping one.
That way they might stay alive.

With the first gray light of dawn, they
hitched the mules to the wagon and went on.
They all agreed that it was useless to send out
a scout. No self-respecting Apache would touch

22

a scout. They would want the men he was scouting for. So they did the only thing they could do—stayed close to the wagon, watched the rocks and the height above them, while they kept their rifles ready. If the Indians were near, most likely the first warning they would have would be a man shot out of the saddle or a downed mule. All they could rely on was their own speed of reaction and the fact that it was likely that the deadliness of their repeating rifles was in their favor against savages who were not so well armed and who were possibly short on ammunition.

Ben Goodall was troubling Arch. Maybe he troubled Mel too, but Arch did not know, for Mel gave no sign. Ben was too tensed, with a sort of strained eagerness on his face, as if he would welcome the sight of an Apache. Arch guessed the man now lived to kill Indians after what had happened to him.

Mel Dawford rode as untidily in the saddle as ever, appearing to be casual, his eyes never ceasing to search the country around him, his rifle on his lap, lines slack, guiding his gaunt sorrel with his knees. He and the horse were old partners and knew each others moods.

The iron tyres of the wagon made an awful

racket now they were into rocky country and it seemed that the whole world was filled with the sound. No Indian within mile could have been deaf to it. It got on Arch's nerves. He also felt as if he were the only target in the area, perched up there on the wagon seat. Every stride the mules took, he felt that when a hidden marksman fired, he would be the one aimed at. It was a fear that grew on him. He wanted to be able to see all around him, but the canvas cover of the wagon restricted his view.

But they reached noon without anything happening and they had climbed a good way. The saddle was now out of sight behind an intervening hill, but they were headed for it in as straight a line as they could keep. The going was often rough in the extreme and often Arch had to dismount and lead the mules. They weren't working well, for they were tired and thirsty. Arch had every sympathy for them, but he kept them on the move, calling to them and cracking the urgent whip about their long ears. At noon they halted briefly to give the animals a breather. An hour and they pushed on again, all of them feeling the intense heat and the lack of water.

Ben said: "Don't fret. We'll be drinkin' our fill before dark."

Gloomily, Mel remarked: "If the Indians ain't sittin' on the *ojo*. That'd be like 'em. They spot us an' they know for certain where we're headed an' they wait for us."

Ben laughed.

"Then we'll kill Indians," he said, "before we drink. That should work up a real thirst."

They climbed steadily and the heat started to recede. As they went higher, so the fierceness of summer was left behind. Brush appeared and a little coarse grass blessed their sight with green. They passed sparse timber. The three men were more cheerful and even the mules started to perk up.

In the middle of the afternoon, Mel rode up alongside Arch and said: "Maybe we should stop here." They stopped and stared up at the saddle which was in view now. "I'm goin' up on foot to take a look around."

Arch didn't like that.

"Did we ought to split up?" he asked.

"If the Indians are at the water," Mel said, "we can't go rollin' in there with a wagon."

That seemed to make sense at the time.

"I'll go," Ben said.

"Naw," said Mel, "this needs pussyfeet. I got 'em."

They both knew that Mel, in spite of his bulk, was a good tracker and could move as silently as a cat. He took off his gun-belt, rolled it around his gun and put it in the wagon. Then he took off his boots and put on a pair of Apache boots that would ensure his silence. He tied his horse to the rear of the wagon and was ready to go.

"Watch out for yourself," Arch said.

"Maybe I won't be back till dark," Mel told him. "Don't wait too long for me. Say a couple of hours past dawn, then you pull out."

"All right," Arch told him. "Sing out before you come in or you might get lead up your butt."

Mel grinned briefly and set off through the rocks. Inside a few minutes, he was out of sight. Ben dismounted and tied his horse. He and Arch unhitched the mules and tied them, they rinsed their mouths out and drank a little water themselves. They then sat one each side of the wagon, watching the country, their rifles in their hands.

Night found them still there and Mel had not returned. Ben agreed to sleep first. He lay under the wagon while Arch kept watch. It was a nerve-racking watch, for he felt certain that there were Indians near. But nothing happened and he awoke Ben at midnight to relieve him.

Arch didn't sleep much. He seemed to close his eyes now and then only to wake in sudden alarm with the feeling that there was an Indian near him. He would feel for his rifle and then lie in his blanket listening before he dozed off again. He finally crawled out from under the wagon an hour before dawn and said to Ben: "Mel not back yet?"

"No," Ben said, "an' I can't say I like it."

Almost as he spoke there came a soft call from out of the dark. Both men tensed and lifted their rifles.

The call came again.

"Hell," Ben whispered, "that could be anythin' or anybody."

They waited, not daring to call back in case they were giving their position away to some savage hidden in the darkness. But one of the mules snorted and there didn't seem much sense in keeping silent.

Arch called softly: "That you, Mel?"

"Yeah. Comin' in."

They heard the sound of his approach a moment later and then he was beside them.

"Christ," he said, "that was some night."

"What happened?" Ben asked.

"Nothin'. That's just it. Nothin'. I didn't see a damn thing. I drank from the *ojo*. Not hide or hair of a 'Pache. But they're up there. As sure as there's a God in heaven they watched me all the time."

Ben said: "You can't be sure."

"I can't be sure," Mel agreed. "There wasn't sign of any kind. They'd cleaned the place up. But they was there. I been around Indians too long to be fooled. I could *feel* Indian."

They all stayed still where they were, thinking, Arch and Ben knowing that Mel knew Indians, yet doubt in their minds.

Ben said: "This is a hell of a note. Do we turn back because you *feel* Indians?"

"We can't turn back," Mel said. "We came for water. We knew there was a good chance of 'em bein' up here an' we still came for water. We have to go on."

"We don't stand a chance of gettin' through 'em with a wagon," Arch said.

"We knew that before we started," Mel said.

28

"But we started just the same. We don't have a choice. We have to go on."

"Yeah," Arch said, a chill settling down his spine. "We have to."

Ben said: "All they have to do is knock over a mule an' we're a sittin' target. They don't have to do nothin' else but hit a mule an' we're finished."

"There's the Winchesters," Mel said. "They don't have nothin' like *them*."

Arch said: "What's the good of talkin' about it. We go on an' thars the end of it."

"I reckon," Mel said.

They each consumed the contents of a tin of tomatoes as they waited for the dawn. Mel filled his pipe, but he wouldn't fire it till light came. As soon as there was a glimmer of light, they hitched up the mules, wanting to get on the move, not able to bear the waiting any longer.

Arch climbed up onto the seat and thought: *Maybe they'll shoot a mule first off or maybe they'll shoot me*. Right now it seemed to be better to be broke than dead. He was just thirty-two and he reckoned there was a lot of life he hadn't seen and now would never get around to seeing.

The mules' breath vaporised in the cold

morning air. They were thirsty and ornery and they hit their collars raggedly when he cracked his whip and bawled at them. The mountains threw back the sounds mockingly. Arch wondered how many Apache ears heard him.

The way narrowed with rocks seeming to lean in on the wagon from either side and Arch saw an Indian behind every one he passed. Mel clattered by and pushed a little ahead. Ben fell back to the rear of the wagon. The heavy vehicle swayed, pitched and jolted over the rocks and Arch prayed that an axle wouldn't go. That was all they need now—a broken axle. The mere thought of it made Arch sweat.

The saddle came in sight, reared high above them. They fought their way on toward it, the mules straining at their collars and Arch making the whip sing. They lurched and strained on their way for what seemed hours, resting every now and then to give the overworked mules a breather. The men spoke seldom and then, unreasonably, in low voices. They watched the heights above them, probed the rocks and the brush near them with their eyes, ready to shoot at anything. By noon they reached the saddle and to Arch's and Ben's surprise found themselves travelling across a pleasantly green

meadow. The place was like a highland paradise, fringed by trees and with a soft and
peaceful appearance that seemed to give the lie
to their fears. To Arch it was a wonderful relief
to find himself in an open space with a couple of
hundred yards between himself and a possible
hidden enemy. The mules perked up at once
and pulled with a will. They could smell water.

Mel led the way on his roan horse at a brisk
walk, heading for a cluster of rocks and willow
trees on the further side of the meadow.
Peaceful the place might look, but Mel seemed
to be a-jitter with nerves. He never seemed to
look in one direction for more than a second.
His head swung this way and that, as if he were
certain that the Indians were somewhere
around, but he did not know exactly where.

When he reached the rocks, he stepped down
from the saddle and called: "Get the team
watered, boys." He ground-hitched his horse
and started climbing the rocks.

Arch jumped down from the wagon and ran
into the rocks and there in front of him was the
"eye' steadily pumping out crystal clear water
from the bowels of the earth. It was like a
miracle. He ran forward, fell on his face and
drank deeply. His whole body sang with relief.

He got to his feet, wiping water over his face with the palm of his hand. Ben passed him and got down to drink. Arch went back to the team and started unhitching them. They were going frantic to get at the water. He glanced up and saw Mel up in the rocks with his rifle held at the ready. Turning his head, he saw Ben walking back toward him. Arch had the two leaders free and he let them go to race to the water. The rest of the team started fighting to follow. He started on the next pair.

Ben called: "Arch."

Arch turned.

At first he could see nothing wrong. Ben was standing still with his right hand at his left shoulder. Then he took a jerky unsteady pace forward and dropped to one knee. Arch saw that there was an arrow sticking in the rear of one shoulder. His eyes flickered up to Mel who was staring in the opposite direction and had noticed nothing.

"Mel," he yelled.

Mel snapped around, crouched as still as stone for a moment, then slapped the butt of the Winchester into his shoulder and fired into the rocks below him.

Ben fell on his face, then reared himself to

his feet and turned toward the rocks, trying to raise his rifle. Arch saw something bright flit from one rock to another. A gun boomed from beyond Ben and Mel came leaping down from his height like a great unwieldy goat.

It seemed to Arch that he stood there for a long time, not seeing anything but his two friends. It was like being a part of a fantastic dream—Ben standing now, still with the arrow sticking out of his shoulder, firing into the rocks, Mel now crouched over the Winchester pumping shots as fast as he could move his hand, empties flying out like bright stars around him.

Then Arch managed to move. He charged for the seat of the wagon where he had left his repeater, snatched it up and legged it toward the rocks. Mel was yelling like an insane man, slowly moving in toward the rocks. Arch at once saw that Mel, once in possession of the water, didn't mean to give it up. The meaning of Mel's shouts were that they were to charge the rocks and clear the Indians out of them. Mel's respect for the Apache did not seem to equal Arch's.

There was no time for thought or fear. Arch continued to run in toward the rocks. Ben too was now going slowly in toward the water, shooting as he went. Arch passed him, glimpsed black smoke among the rocks and knew the Indians were shooting back. There seemed to be a hell of a racket going on, yells, screams and shots filled the air. He sighted an Indian firing at Mel, slammed the Winchester into his shoulder and triggered off a shot. He missed and worked the lever. The empty tinkled onto rock and he went to fire again only to find that his target was no longer in sight. Lead hummed past him. He swung around and saw a man running. A tangle of coarse black hair, a crimson head rag, the flash of white teeth in a brown face. The man sighted him, stopped and raised his rifle. Arch fired.

The bullet knocked the man backward and he dropped his rifle. Arch levered another round into the breech. The Indian drew a knife from his belt, grimaced with pain and started forward with his face contorted by the effort. His breast was covered with blood.

What do you have to do to stop one of these bastards? Arch asked himself.

He aimed as carefully as he could with a yelling savage charging straight at him and fired.

He hit the man in mid-stride. The fellow leapt high in the air and fell to the ground. He kicked a little and lay still.

Then, startlingly, it was silent.

Arch looked at Mel. He was panting as if he had run a long way and the sweat was pouring down his face. Arch switched his glance to Ben. He was standing stooped a little with the arrow still decorating him.

Mel said: "For God's sake take that thing outa Ben," and stalked into the rocks.

Arch walked over to Ben. His mind was still on the Indians. He couldn't believe they weren't still there in the rocks, watching him.

Ben said: "Break it off behind. The head's almost through out front."

Arch laid down his rifle on a rock. He got his hands on the haft of the arrow and felt Ben tense. He hesitated.

Ben said: "Hurry it up, we don't have all day."

Arch put two counter-pressures on the haft and did it carefully so that he wouldn't give Ben too much pain. The man went rigid on tip-toe when Arch snapped the arrow in half.

"Christ," he whispered.

He was white to the mouth, he seemed to

sway a little. After he had plucked ineffectually at the arrow head for a moment, he said: "Get the damn thing out, man."

Arch went around to the front of him, took the tip of the arrowhead in his right hand and pressed against Ben's shoulder with the left.

In the rocks, Mel fired a single shot.

Arch pulled on the arrowhead. It resisted for a moment, then came away freely in his fingers, followed by a gush of blood. Ben clutched at him blindly with one hand and clung there for a moment.

"Easy, boy," Arch said.

Ben didn't speak. His eyes were shut and his teeth were clenched in a grin of pain.

Mel came back, shouting to Arch angrily.

"He's blood all over, man. Patch him up, then get him up here to watch the rocks, while we load up with water."

Arch said: "Ben ain't goin' to be much good to us for a while, Mel. He's hurt bad."

Mel snapped: "He's got an arrow in him. Plenty of men have had arrows in 'em."

"He can hardly stand."

Mel glared in a kind of simmering fury.

"He's gotta stand. You an' me load the water and he gets up there an' he covers us."

Ben sat down suddenly, shaking violently and looking ashen.

"He's right," he said. "Quit yammering, Arch. We're wastin' time."

Mel stomped back into the rocks.

"Come back near the wagon," Arch said, picking up his rifle. He helped Ben to his feet and they made it to the wagon. Ben sat down with his back to a wheel and Arch found an old shirt in his warbag. Tearing it into strips, he rolled one into a pad and held this hard against the blood-oozing wound. Ben held the pad while Arch bound it into place. Arch hoped the arrow had been clean, but he knew he probably hoped in vain. He had got the last knot on the bandage tight when there came a flurry of shots from the rocks.

He picked up his rifle and started forward on the run. At first when he reached the rocks, he couldn't see anything. He passed the eye and caught sight of Mel crouched behind a boulder, firing. Something sang past Arch and hit a rock with a *clunk*. He threw himself down, saw a brown shoulder and started firing and levering. Time became an uncertain thing and he did not know how long he was there, firing and sweating, trying to stop those silently flitting figures, never knowing if he had hit one. Then, once again, the place was weighed down with silence.

Mel laughed without humor.

"That should change their minds for a piece." He raised his voice in a shout.

"Ben, get up here."

Ben staggered up to them. He looked terrible and Arch was full of wonder that he could stay on his feet at all.

Mel said: "Get forward a mite, Ben, and hold 'em while we tote water. We'll be out of here in no time at all."

Ben went past them like a ghost.

Arch and Mel walked back to the wagon. For a moment, they debated what to do with their rifles while they loaded water. There were no slings on the weapons and they couldn't carry them while they worked. They decided to put them in the wagon. This they did and man-handled the first barrel from the wagon. Arch rolled this toward the rocks, while Mel got the second one down. Arch left his barrel by the edge of the water and passed Mel rolling the second.

Mel snarled: "Hurry it up, for Crissake."

Arch broke into a run. He rolled another

half-dozen barrels from the bed of the wagon and by the time Mel had come back he was on his way with a second.

The Indians still seemed to be quiet and while he toiled, Arch's mind never left them once. All the time he was thinking that Ben had passed out in the rocks and they were totally unprotected. They got all the barrels at the eye. They had two funnels and two coffee pots and those were the only aids they had to fill the barrels. It was going to be slow work. They set up two barrels, knocked out the bungs and started filling with the coffee pots. All was still quiet. They worked as fast as water would flow. They worked for a half-hour and then Arch walked into the rocks and called: "You all right, Ben?"

"I'm all right," Ben answered and Arch started back toward the pool.

A bright flutter of cloth caught his eye. A mule screamed and went down. Arch saw the flash of the knife. There was an Indian among the mules. Another appeared around the rear of the wagon.

The rifles, was the thought that screamed itself in Arch's mind.

He broke into a run, tearing his Remington

from its holster and calling to Mel. He went past Mel, yelling to attract the attention of the Indian at the mules, to stop him killing another animal. The man turned, knife in hand. Arch didn't dare shoot in case he hit the animals. The man at the rear of the wagon fired his rifle from the hip. Black smoke blossomed from its muzzle and something plucked viciously at Arch's sleeve. He ran on and the man at the mules rushed to meet him. Arch had a momentary vision of bared teeth, wild animal eyes and a painted face. He halted, fired and had the vision obliterated by the smoke of his pistol. He leapt sideways to get out of the smoke and faced the man with the rifle. It was a single-shot breech-loading carbine and the man had no time to load. He ran silently, raising the weapon clubwise. Arch cocked, fired and missed, dodged out of the smoke again and heard a gun roar behind him. The Indian with the rifle seemed to trip over his own feet, hit the ground on his shoulder and somersaulted.

Arch switched his eyes to the man who had killed the mule. He squirmed on the ground in an ecstasy of agony. Mel fired again and he lay still.

Mel laughed.

"That should teach 'em it don't pay," he said.

The mules were going crazy. The one with its throat cut was kicking its partner as it lay on the ground. Mel walked up to it and shot it through the head. It gave a final kick and lay still.

Arch stood still for a moment, feeling drained.

Then he pulled himself together, put his gun away and cut the dead mule free. He moved the team with great difficulty away from the dead animal and tried to quieten them down. Mel inspected the two fallen Apaches and declared them dead. He went back to filling barrels. Arch got the team fairly quiet, then moved them almost up to the eye. The lone leader was no good on his lonesome, so Arch cut him loose and tied him with the horses at the rear of the wagon. Then he joined Mel and got to work with the coffee pot.

As soon as they had two barrels full, they got them aboard the wagon. This was a considerable chore and it took the stuffing out of them. Water was heavy stuff. They could have done with Ben unwounded and hale. But there wasn't time to take a breather, they set up two more

41

barrels and started filling them. They worked for an hour or more without sight or sound of the Indians. They uttered scarcely a word, except to swear, and worked feverishly. Once or twice they heard a shot from Ben, but nothing more happened. Finally, around noon, they had all the barrels filled and aboard the wagon. Once it was done, they could scarcely believe that they had accomplished so much. Mel must have been right, Arch thought. The Indians must have realised that it didn't pay to tangle with these whitemen at their water.

Arch called: "Ben, come on in."

Ben appeared through the rocks. He walked hesitantly like a man in a dream.

Arch said: "Do you think you could drive, Ben?"

"I've gotta," Ben said.

Wearily, he climbed up onto the driving seat and took up the lines. Mel came from the pool with several canteens full of water. Arch went to the pool, lay down and drank till he almost burst. That ration should last him awhile. He had heard men claim that one should take little water aboard in desert country and grow used to doing without. But he didn't believe it.

Drink all you could when you could, was his motto.

He rose, wiped his face, eyed the surrounding rocks for a moment and walked back to the wagon. He untied his bay from the tailboard of the wagon and stepped into the saddle. Mel got into the saddle and Ben started the mules. The reduced team fought the increased weight, then the wheels turned. Arch took the right-hand side of the wagon and Mel the left. Ben swung the vehicle in an arc across the meadow and headed back through the saddle. The mules hit a steady walk and he kept them to it with a ready whip. They would never be able to hit a faster pace on the flat pulling such a load.

Halfway across the grass, something made Arch turn his head. He pivoted the bay and yelled: "Ben—behind!"

4

THEY came out of the rocks like brightly-colored birds, their loose shirt-tails fluttering, their ponies being beaten into a hard gallop.

Ben called: "What is it?"

Arch shouted: "Keep goin'."

The bay started to dance with excitement. Arch spoke to it in hoarse rider's language to steady it. Mel's mount started pitching unexpectedly and the air rang with the rider's obscenities.

Arch could hear the sound of the approaching horses' hoofs. One of the Indians was yelling. It sounded like the yipping of a wild animal. There were, Arch saw, no more than nine or ten of them. But for his book that made nine or ten too many. He levered a round into the breech of the Winchester and swung down from the saddle. Sternly, he told the bay to stand. Glancing at Mel, he saw that his partner had done the same thing.

"Now," Mel called.

They started firing together, pouring their repeater fire into the oncoming riders. Two first-class riflemen firing into a head-on target. They couldn't miss. There was a sort of gross injustice about it. They fired quickly and steadily and the Indians burst asunder like a flight of quail, lining out and running ahead so that they came thundering along on either side of the two whitemen. Arch and Mel abruptly stopped firing, piled into the saddle, whirled their horses as one man and spurred furiously after the wagon for which the Indians were heading.

There followed a crazy whirlwind five minutes of guiding the horses by their knees, firing from the saddle of a running horse at targets that flitted uncertainly before their eyes. There was no time for thought. They did the only thing they could do, to get between the Indians and the wagon, to fire and lever as fast as they knew how. Arch saw the mule at the rear of the wagon go down. For a second he seemed to be surrounded by Indians. One of them struck at him, he dropped the Winchester, nearly fell from the saddle and tore the Remington from leather. A face appeared beneath him, black hair tangled, eyes glaring wildly through it. He fired point-blank and it was plucked away from his sight. Then he was alone and alongside the wagon.

He turned the bay, saw a fleeing Indian, fired and missed.

Movement to the right caught his eye.

Mel was in trouble.

His horse was down and Mel lay with one foot caught in a stirrup-iron. Arch rammed the spurs home as he saw the Indian heading for the fallen man, whooping in with savage delight.

He threw up his gun, cocked and squeezed the trigger. An empty click was the result. The Indian tried to ride his pony over Mel, but the animal shied away and swerved to one side. The rider tried to roughly turn it, but it fought him. Mel got his foot free and staggered to his feet. Smoke appeared at the end of the Indian's arm and Arch knew that he was armed with a revolver. Mel threw his hands up to his face and started to walk blindly in a circle.

Arch drove the bay into the flank of the Indian pony. The animal squealed and went over under the superior weight. The rider jumped clear, was on his feet in a second, gun in hand.

Again, there was no time for thought or fear.

It was all a rush of breathless action. Arch jumped the bay into the Indian, the man dodged to one side, fired and missed. Arch launched himself from the saddle, blindly. How he hit the Apache, he never knew, but they both went down in a tangle of arms and legs. For a second there was a reek of bear fat in Arch's nostrils. This was blasted from him as the Indian fired his gun. Then Arch was coughing on cordite and smashing insanely at the man with the barrel of the Remington.

He was astride the man, pounding at his head. The Indian struck him across the face with his forearm, twisted violently and threw him clear. Arch reared to his feet and charged. The Indian went away before him, using the force of the charge to hurl the whiteman over the top of him. Arch thought he had never hit solid ground so hard and for a moment he lay like a man stunned. Fear hit him then and fear is a mighty livener. He rolled as the Indian fired and heard the bullet strike the sod near his head. The same fear then propelled him to his feet. There was nothing to do but charge again to stop the man shooting once more. This Arch did, swinging the Remington. The Indian backed up from him, grimacing himself with fear now. The sight gave Arch new strength. He missed the man's head and brought the barrel down hard on his shoulder. The Indian lurched away from him and Arch followed relentlessly.

Backing up, the Apache raised his gun to fire and brought the hammer down on an empty cartridge case. He thumbed and triggered again without success and then Arch was on him. But he never got a blow home. Suddenly, the man turned and took to his heels.

Arch thought: *My God, an Apache ran from me.*

He turned.

Mel was sitting on the ground wiping blood from his eyes.

Further on, the wagon had halted and Ben was firing from the seat at some retreating Indians. Two ponies lay dead on the ground and near them lay an Apache. Arch walked over to Mel and took a close look at him.

"It ain't nothin'," Mel said. "Ball musta grazed my head."

Arch said: "Get in the wagon, we can't wait around here all day."

Mel got to his feet.

"I ain't leaving the saddle. It's a good saddle."

Watching the Indians riding away into cover, Arch said angrily: "Get into the wagon, man." Mel started to wander away. Arch stopped him with: "Take your rifle. I can't carry every durned thing."

Mel picked up his rifle and went on to the wagon. Hastily, but with some difficulty, Arch got the saddle and bridle off the dead horse and toted them to the wagon. Then he whistled the bay and the animal came trotting up. He swung into the saddle and got moving as the wagon rolled forward.

He came alongside the wagon and Ben said: "We showed 'em. By God, didn't we just shown 'em." He laughed dryly. "They been pushin' us around for years, burnin' an' killin', chasin' troops all over the country like they was scared kids an' now the three of us really showed 'em. I killed one. So that's two they owe me an' I'll have 'em before we hit Crewsville."

From the wagon bed came Mel's voice.

"You'll have your chance, man. They ain't finished with us yet. You thought? If they're Juanito's boys, there ain't many of 'em. There's more some place an' when they hear about us they're goin' to come a-runnin'. We ain't even started yet."

Ben turned on the wagon seat. There was delight on his pale face.

"Suits me," he said. "The more that come, the more I cut down."

Arch came up around the rear of the wagon and looked in on Mel. He saw that his partner had tied his bandanna around his head. Blood still trickled down his face. He looked like a slightly drunken pirate. He grinned.

"Boy," he said, "we goin' to make it."

Arch said: "We ain't there yet."

They rolled across the meadow and into high timber. Arch went ahead and Mel watched their rear. The heavily laden wagon rocked and rolled over the rough surface, the mules strained more willingly than on the outward journey now that they had drunk their fill. Arch rode with his chin on either shoulder, wary and jumpy. Slowly, they worked their way over the saddle without sight of an Indian and started the steep descent. Ben had to use the brake frequently, for often the wagon threatened to run away. There was a lot of cursing and the animals were having a rough time of it. Only when they were down into the more arid and rocky country did

Arch realise that scarcely a morsel of food had passed their lips all day. He drew some jerky from his pocket and chewed on it. Dark overtook them with its startling suddenness while they were still in the foothills.

They halted, unhitched the mules and fed them tied to the wagon. They then slept one at a time, letting Ben get into a blanket first. Arch was the last to sleep and he had no sooner put his head down than somebody was shaking him by the shoulder.

He sat up abruptly, finding it still dark.

5

MEL'S voice came. "It's near dawn. If they're comin', we're near the time."
Arch rose with his blanket and rifle in his hands, threw the blanket into the back of the wagon and joined the other two hitching the mules. They had that done when dawn came. It wasn't much fun fighting reluctant mules into place, expecting an arrow or a bullet to come out of the darkness at any moment. It was so dark that they could scarcely see the animals they were handling. Mel was kicked and cursed the air foul. Ben thought it was funny and laughed. Arch wasn't in the mood to think anything funny. He was thinking of the next few minutes when silent forms would come slinking through the rocks at them.

When the mules were hitched, Arch stood with his horse at the heads of the mules. If there was shooting, they wanted the animals under control. Ben took his place on the driving seat and Mel clambered into the wagon to cover the rear. Arch split his watch between the rocks and the sky. He watched the cold finger of dawn stretching across the heavens. The mules were uneasy. The bay stood patiently. Arch knew that the Indians could be really close, ready for the quick rush, the stab and the gunshot. It could all be over in a matter of seconds. The whole idea of making their fortunes with the run to Crewsville seemed the craziest idea of his life.

Suddenly, he could see the rocks at the side of the trail and the fact startled him.

The bay jumped.

Arch gave the rocks a glance in front of him and saw nothing, then turned his head and looked behind. Nothing. He thought to take his cue from the bay. Its ears were forward, head up and he was watching the rocks to the right of the trail. It shied and swung its rump around, barging into Arch and nearly knocking him from his feet. The mules took alarm, one of them tried to turn and stepped over the traces. Arch caught a glimpse of movement among the rocks. He tried to steady the bay with a word as he brought the Winchester to his shoulder and fired.

There was a sudden rush of almost silent movement and it seemed that there were figures all around him. Mel and Ben both started shooting. The sound of the gunfire echoed and re-echoed among the rocks. The mules went berserk. As the bay moved again, Arch was caught between the horse and the frantic lead mules. He batted the horse's head aside and ducked under it. As he came upright again, he was face to face with an Indian.

He fired the Winchester point-blank.

The man disappeared in the uncertain light, but Arch never knew if he had hit him.

Mel's roar came from the rear.

"Get movin'."

Ben's whip cracked and he started howling at the mules. Arch darted along the side of the team as the mules hit their collars and tried to free the mule that had stepped over the traces, yelling for Ben to hold it a moment. Something hummed past his head and thudded into the rump of the mule. The animal tried to rear and went out of its head. Arch managed to free it of the traces. Ben was still trying to get the animals on the move and they surged past Arch. They ran into the bay and there was a hell of a mix-up. Arch ran along the team, grabbed one of the bay's trailing lines and pulled it out of the way of the lunging mule-team. A gun went off near him and he thought he felt its blast. For one confused second, he didn't know whether he was hit or not. The wagon started to rock by him, he made a clumsy effort to get aboard the bay and the animal jumped forward, almost taking him from his feet. Something struck the horn of the saddle a violent blow and the horse staggered. Arch managed to get a foot into a stirrup-iron and heaved himself into the saddle.

An Indian came into view, leaping up onto a rock, standing for a moment to fire at the wagon. Awkwardly, Arch leaned forward to gather up a lost line, managed to reach it and straightened up to take a shot at the Indian only to find him gone. He kicked the spurs into the bay and the animal broke into a startled run.

Suddenly, there was an Indian running beside him, matching the horse stride by stride. This was on the right side and Arch's right foot was not in the stirrup-iron. As the man sprang in close to him, he brought the toe of his boot into the man's chest, knocking him sideways and off-balance. The Indian seemed to catch himself up and started to swerve in again. Arch turned the bay abruptly and ran the animal into the man. What damage he did, he didn't know, but the man went down, the bay continued its circle and ran on after the wagon.

Ben had the mules going at a crazy pace with the wagon bouncing and swaying wildly. It struck a rock and seemed to leap high in the air. A horseman appeared to its right, crouching low in the crude saddle, firing as he charged. Mel blazed away at him over the tailboard of the wagon and he swerved away.

Arch looked back over his shoulder and saw three men coming after him on foot, running as only an Apache could run. He had heard of them running down horsemen over short distances and now he believed it.

He brought the bay to a sliding halt. The animal reared as it turned and as soon as its forefeet were down on the ground, Arch had the Winchester at his shoulder and was levering and firing. Again he did not know if he made a hit and he didn't wait to find out. He turned the willing bay again and once more used the spurs. The Indians had leapt into cover on either side of the trail, but in spite of the panic they had shown, it did not stop them from sending shots after him.

It seemed that for a moment they were clear of Indians. They clattered and slammed through a narrow passage between two giant rocks and the trail dropped away before them. Ben must have forgotten about the brake. He let the mules have their heads and kept them moving with the whip to keep them ahead of the speeding wagon. Mel was bounced around like a shuttlecock in the rear. Arch wouldn't have been surprised to have seen him tossed over the tailboard at any minute.

They ran on like this for the craziest two miles or so that Arch had ever experienced; then they hit the flat and kept on going. Every time the mules tried to slack off, Ben livened them up with his whip and some choice curses. Arch took the bay up alongside him and shouted: "You tryin' to kill them mules?"

Ben yelled back: "I'm fixin' so them 'Paches don't kill me."

"There ain't an Indian in sight. Ease up."

Ben took a look backward and Mel roared at him that he had broken every damn bone in his body and was he satisfied now? Ben slackened the pace and brought the mules down to a brisk trot.

Arch stopped the bay and took a good look at the hills behind them. Nothing moved.

Satisfied that for the moment the danger had passed, he rode on after the wagon.

The mules were bushed. They had come down to a plodding walk. Ben, not feeling too good, now lay among the barrels which had been secured with ropes as soon as there had been an opportunity. Mel drove. They had rested at noon and watered the stock, now they expected to sight the laagered wagons any moment. Arch rode ahead and breasted a ridge. Halting the bay, he shaded his eyes and caught sight of the white wagon covers. He waved a signal to Mel who raised his hand in response.

Arch took another careful look at the wagons.

Something was wrong down there. At first, he couldn't see what it was, but it suddenly came to him that one wagon was without its cover.

Mel brought the water-wagon slowly up behind him, stopped for a moment on top of the ridge and surveyed the scene below him.

"My God," Mel said, "they been hit."

Ben got to his feet and stared over Mel's shoulder. They all stayed still, staring, uneasiness coming over all three of them.

Ben said: "This could mean anything."

"I'll go in and take a look. Maybe the Indians have the whole train."

Mel nodded.

"It's possible. I don't see any of the boys."

They were silent for a moment in a kind of dread.

Arch started the bay forward, but Mel called to him and said: "You crazy? Fire a shot."

Arch triggered the Winchester.

For a few seconds nothing happened, then a lone figure rose up in the wagon without the cover. He waved them in.

"Is that a whiteman?" Ben asked.

Arch told him: "I can't see. Only one way to tell." He urged the bay forward at a trot. Mel called after him: "Watch out for yourself."

Arch levered a round into the breech of the rifle. He kept his eyes on the wagons. As the distance shortened another and another figure appeared. He slowed his pace. One of the men shouted.

That was Charlie Garth. Arch sighed with relief. He turned in the saddle and beckoned Mel on. When he reached the wagons and stepped down wearily from the saddle, there were men all around him. He looked from face to face. Most of them were black with burned powder.

"What happened here?" he asked.

Garth said: "We was jumped. At night. Don't nobody never tell me red-sticks don't fight at night. They shot the hell out of us and used fire-arrows to boot. You boys knew what you was up to when you took off for the hills."

"Sure," Arch said dryly, "we had a real good time."

The men turned and looked at the approaching wagon and one said: "That why you only have four mules?"

Garth demanded: "You get the water?"

"We got it," Arch said and they all brightened. He knew they were not all here. "How many was hit?"

Garth told him: "Henry Burrows was killed. Damn nigh blew his head off. Art Slogan got a knife in his belly. He'll live—maybe."

A man said: "It could of been worse."

"It was the rifles that saved us," Garth said. "If it wasn't for the repeaters, they'd of made mince-meat of us."

The wagon rolled up and the men rushed forward. They stopped when they saw that both Mel and Ben had been hit. There were questions and answers about the fighting for a few minutes before their thirst got the better of them. Charlie Garth came forward and started giving out water. As soon as their thirsts were quenched they saw to the stock. It was upwards of an hour before they were finished and Mel was going around roaring for the men to hitch the teams. A new team was put on the water-wagon, some supplies were put aboard and then with no more than three hours of daylight left to them they rolled again.

Mel was in the saddle again, riding up and down the train, growling for drivers to keep up. He found Arch once at the rear of the train watching the back-trail. He came up alongside and grinned cheerful through his growing whiskers.

"We goin' to make it, boy."

Arch said: "I don't know if we're goin' to. But we got to."

Mel said with unaccustomed somberness: "We lost a man dead, Arch. We have to face a widder woman when we get back to Tucson."

Arch nodded.

"I know," he said and did not relish the chore.

6

MEN and animals were bushed, the water was almost gone. The men were red-eyed from lack of sleep through keeping double-guards and standing to at dawn. The wounded man had died the day before and brought the death roll to two. Yet now there was an almost cheerful air about the men. They knew their ordeal was almost over and minute by minute as they neared Crewsville, the chances of being hit by the Indians again grew less.

Arch rode on ahead, came on a tired bay to what he reckoned was the last ridge and there stood the town spread out before him. He sat still in the saddle for a moment, looking at it. It was scattered untidily around the outcrop of rocks that seemed to have been thrown by a careless gargantuan hand. It was dusty, hot, airless and, he knew from experience, the haven of every last ruffian of the frontier. In his mind, he always thought of it as the last frontier. Here had come all the flotsam of the West that had been moved on from the now fairly law-abiding towns of Texas, Colorado, Utah and other western states. Yet to him now, it looked like paradise. It not only meant that Mel and he had accomplished what they had set out to do, but that he could wash, shave and eat a good meal. His mind went for a black moment to the two men who had died and he knew that he could be thankful that there had not been more.

He waited for the wagons to come up with him and then slowly led the way down from the ridge and on toward town. They had been sighted. That was soon evident by the sudden appearance of riders on the outskirts. One light-hearted young fool started shooting his gun into the air; across the arid plain sounded a thin cheer. Horsemen came galloping toward them. The mules pricked up their ears and the men were straining to see the town that they thought they might never see.

The first horseman was a ragged-assed cowhand on a rawboned piece of crowbait. He rode at Arch, halted and spun his horse with a fine air of bravado and yelled: "You from Tucson, mister?" Arch affirmed that he was. "Can a man ask what you have in them wagons back there?"

63

"Sure can," Arch told him. "We have everythin' a man or woman needs. An' we'll be tradin' at the Forstel corral this evening."

The boy yipped and spurred his horse, racing with the news toward town. Another rider took his place, a sober man in a brown store suit, brown derby straight on head. He was sweating in the heat and suffering from the short ride. Something urgent had brought him out a-horseback in the sun.

"You're Kelso, ain't you, sir?" he demanded, wiping the sweat from his face, removing the derby and setting it back in place with a wince.

"That's right."

"I'm Snyder. John S. Snyder of the Snyder Emporium. Sell everything from a needle to a plough-share—rifles, boots, hats, pretties for the ladies, you name it, we have it." He looked hastily over his shoulder to see how close the next rider was. "The story reached town you were headed this way with supplies, all kinds of supplies." He gasped breath into his fat chest and hurried on. "I'm here to do business. I sell fair and I buy fair. I'll buy you out, sir, lock, stock and barrel."

Arch smiled.

"We ain't sellin'," he said.

"Not selling?" Snyder looked aghast. "You mean you came all this way for nothing? It seems hardly credible . . . I mean . . . You're in business, aren't you?"

"On our own account."

Mel brought up the first wagon and halted, listening. He looked hugely amused. Arch winked at him.

"I don't seem to remember you having a location in town, Kelso."

"We don't."

"But you say you're in business."

"We'll sell from the Forstel corral."

Snyder looked aghast.

"I assure you, sir, the business folk of Crewsville would never permit that. No, sir."

Mel said: "You ride back an' tell 'em, mister, before you plumb melt away."

Snyder gave him a venomous glance.

"State a price, gentlemen," he said. "I'll pay anything reasonable. I'll take everything you have off your hands. You won't regret it."

Mel said: "But we'll regret it if'n we don't, huh?"

Snyder looked flustered.

"Face facts," he said. "Crewsville is a tight

65

little town. It don't take too kindly to outsiders coming in and trading regardless."

The second rider was near. He had storekeeper written all over him too. He was a mite thinner than Snyder but he was doing his fair share of sweating. He gave Snyder a hard look.

"Trust you to be here first," he snapped. He beamed on Arch and Mel. "Allow me to introduce myself, gentlemen. Arthur K. Negus, at your service. Owner of the Negus Emporium. Known to the whole town as Honest Art. County commissioner and one of the founder members of this community."

Snyder growled: "I was here first, Negus. You hold your trap till I'm done."

Negus didn't hear.

"Whatever he offered you, gentlemen, I'll up," he said. "I'll pay cash right here and now for all you have carried from Tucson. Hard Yankee dollars. Sell now and go into town with your pockets jingling."

His beaming smile was bright as the sun.

Arch said: "We're tradin' on our own account."

It was Negus' turn to look aghast.

"You can't mean it, sir. You can't. That would never be permitted in Crewsville. It

66

would be a fell blow to the whole trading community. I am sure the marshal would have something to say about that. Reconsider, I beg of you, before you jeopardise your whole enterprise."

Snyder cried: "I told them, Art, but will they listen?"

A third horseman rode up. He was a tall man, clothed in black with long golden hair to his shoulders. He rode a black horse. Arch and Mel both knew him. Once they had served as law officers with him, once they had resided for a night in his jail and once, they suspected, they had had a run-in at night with him when he was lifting a goodly number of Arch's cattle. He was John Stratton.

He reined up, unsmiling and eyed them.

"Howdy, Arch. Ben." They said howdy. Loudly, Snyder and Negus began their complaint. Arch and Mel watched with interest. Mel unobtrusively lifted the Winchester by his side and laid it across his lap. He knew that Stratton hadn't missed the movement.

Marshal Stratton said: "Is what these two gentlemen say true, boys?"

Arch said: "I reckon."

The marshal looked saddened.

"A pity," he said. "You come a long way. You go ahead an' you're liable to be plumb disappointed. It's a cryin' shame."

Arch thought: *Fifty dollars would settle that one's hash. But I'm damned if I do*. He glanced at Mel and saw from his partner's pursed lips and squinting eyes that Mel felt the same way.

Mel said with dangerous quietness: "Think it over, Johnny."

Snyder said: "We have offered these men fair prices."

"Boys," Stratton said, "let's keep this friendly. These two gentlemen are respected traders in the town. They want to play fair with you."

"Johnny," Arch said, "we're all tired. Our tempers ain't too good. We're goin' into town, we're goin' to the Forstel corral and we're goin' to trade from there."

Garth strolled forward from the train and stood off to Stratton's left. He held a shot-gun in his hands. He didn't point it at anybody, but his intentions were plain. Mel shifted the Winchester slightly and its barrel was lined up with the marshal.

Stratton said, through his teeth: "I'm the law in town."

68

"When we break a law," Arch said, "you come a-runnin'. Till we do, stay off'n our necks."

Stratton smiled.

"You'll break a law," he said. "You'd be surprised just how quickly you can break a law in my town."

Mel said: "We'll remember that."

Stratton nodded affably, said: "Do that," and neck-reined his fine horse around. Making angry noises, the two merchants followed him.

Mel, who had appeared calm throughout the conversation, now screwed up his face in rage and disgust.

"That does it," he said. "They got us over a barrel. That lousy son-of-a-bitch Stratton. We can't go back an' they know it. If we go forward they milk us dry."

Garth said: "What if you sell out to those fellers?"

"That's the word—'sell-out'. That's what it'd be. Robbery. Those boys are sharks. With Stratton, they got the town sewed up tight." Arch looked grim. "But they ain't got us sewed up tight."

"They're headed straight for Forstel, right

69

now," Mel said. "In five minutes, they'll have the pressure on him."

Arch said: "We'll get on. We ain't goin' to gain nothin' sitting here gabbing about it."

He turned his horse and led the way slowly toward town. Garth walked back to his wagon and Mel cracked his whip. They rolled slowly on into town.

There were plenty of people there to greet them. It looked like the whole town that wasn't working in the mines was there to see the wagon-train of supplies arrive. A ragged cheer went up. Little boys ran up and down excitedly. A few guns were fired in the air. Men raced forward to throw questions at the drivers—how had they fared on the trip? Had they seen any Indians? Was the water situation bad out on the desert? Slowly, the train pushed its way through the crowd and edged its way down Main. Arch, in the lead, turned aside to the corral and there at the gate was Forstel himself, a big, black-bearded man. Arch and Mel had known him for some years and had always been on friendly terms with him. He looked up at Arch and said: "Howdy, Arch."

"Howdy," Arch said and swung down from

the saddle. He grinned and said: "Got room for us, George. We've come to make your fortune."

Forstel said: "Sorry, Arch. No room."

He could have been speaking the truth. The gate behind him was solid and the old adobe walls of the corral were too high to see over, even from the back of a horse.

Mel halted his team behind Arch and climbed down. He came striding over and greeted Forstel. Arch said: "George says he don't have room for us."

Mel showed surprise.

"This never happened before, did it, George?"

Forstel said: "We never had an Indian uprising before."

Mel smiled widely.

"I think you're being smart, George, ol'-timer. You want a cut. An' why not? Business is business, even between friends."

Forstel moved from one foot to another. He wasn't liking this at all.

"Sorry," he said. "I can't help, Mel. I just don't have the room. That's the truth."

Garth and one or two of the men came up.

"What's the matter, George," Garth demanded. "Stratton get to you."

Forstel flushed.

Angrily, he said: "No call for that kind of talk, Garth. I'm just full up an' that's the end of it."

Arch turned and swung into the saddle again.

"Can't see what anybody's goin' to gain by this," he said. "We have what the town wants and the town's goin' to get it. Come on, boys, we'll camp outside town."

"Sure," Mel said and tramped away to his wagon and picked up the lines. The other men turned and headed back for their wagons. Forstel somberly watched them go.

They had their work cut out to get the teams turned in the street with so many people about, but finally they made it and headed out of town. Arch and Mel saw no sign of the two traders or the marshal. They laagered the wagons at Mel's orders just as if they were in Indian country. The people had followed them and were still full of questions, wanting to know what supplies they had on board and what kind of prices they were asking. Night came on and slowly the people headed back into town. Garth and the men soon had fires going and a meal cooking. The smell of broiling meat and coffee filled the air.

72

Arch said to Mel: "Armed guards out, partner. We have what they all want."

Mel said: "You bet your sweet life."

Doc Dooley leaned on the corral rail and chewed on a straw. He watched the fires near the Kelso and Dawford wagons and the thought of all the things they had aboard their wagons made his mouth water. It also made his hand itch to get at their goods. Doc was a thief by instinct, training and inclination. He was one of those strange creatures who would go to enormous pains to obtain other men's property without paying for it.

The five men with him chewed and smoked, wondering what was going on in his mind, what plan was hatching there. The four brothers all looked alike, all big men with a sweep of fair hair and heavy fair mustaches. They all went in for white linen and black cloth, for highly polished boots and fine carefully tended revolvers which they wore at their right hips. They all had dead cold eyes which glittered only now in the distant firelight over by the laagered wagons.

Doc was weighing the possibilities. He could go in there with the four brothers and Ringus, risk getting hurt for the sake of taking supplies which could be identified later. He could wait for the supplies to be sold and then take the money that had bought them. And that would be a considerable sum, the way prices were rising now in Crewsville. Or, and this was where he hesitated, he could wait and see what happened; wait and see if Kelso and Dawford carried gold out of town. But, he knew, that might mean that he got nothing at all.

He decided. He'd have his cake and eat it, as it were. He'd take the money off the partners and, later, if they did carry gold out of town, he'd take that from them too. And he didn't doubt that he could do it. He had taken on tougher ones than Kelso and Dawford in his time and come out of it with profit.

He chuckled fatly to himself and pushed himself away from the corral fence.

"Ringus, my boy," he said, "you watch that camp. Anythin' special happens, I want to know."

Ringus said: "How long do I stay?"

"Till I tell you to leave."

"Aw, shucks, Doc . . ."

The brothers laughed.

Doc turned and walked into town, the four

tall men trailing behind him. They didn't see anything strange in four big tough gunhands walking like puppy dogs behind a comical figure like Doc.

They were afraid of him.

Mel sat on a barrel head and slapped his belly.

"By God," he said, "I can't wait. I just can't wait."

Arch pulled on his pipe and said: "Why can't you wait? What do you want to get at: the whiskey, the women or all the money we're goin' to make when we sell this little lot?"

Mel grinned amiably.

"Right all along the line. First, whiskey to purge me of dust. Second, a good strong woman to purge me of all the bad thoughts I been havin'. Third, all the money we're goin' to make that'll purge me of bein' broke."

Arch said: "We can't both go into town. One of us has to stay here."

Mel jerked a look at him.

"What in hell do you want to go into town for, man?"

"You ain't the only one with needs."

Mel snorted.

"You don't drink more'n one whiskey,

whorin' ain't in your line a-tall an' I don't recall you havin' no other vices."

"She ain't a vice, she's a virtue."

Mel roared: "You don't mean Martha Dean. You can't. She has a face like a horse."

Arch had heard that before. It didn't faze him. Poker-faced he said softly: "Say that again and I'll knock your teeth down your throat."

"All right, all right," Mel shouted. "I'll give you an hour with Martha. You can't hold hands for more'n an hour. Not even you and Martha. Then I'm out a-whorin'."

Arch slapped his hat on his head, hitched at his gun-belt and said: "An hour will do me fine."

Mel looked at him coyly. "Don't do nothin' I wouldn't do," he said.

"With Martha?" Arch said in mock horror and walked away toward town. As he entered Main, to his plain-bound eyes the lights appeared dazzlingly bright. The place seemed to be full of life and movement, folk on the sidewalk and wheeled traffic on the street. The many saloons on either side of the street were doing a roaring trade. A fight was in progress in front of one of them between a Cornish miner and an Irish laborer who used heads, teeth and feet as much as their hands. A fair crowd watched and shouted encouragement. There was no lawman in evidence. A Chinaman hurried by with small steps, carrying somebody's wash; a painted woman called to him from an open window; a man in a hard hat sold patent medicines from the back of a wagon with a lantern swinging. All this on Main. The town had altered since he was here last.

As he mounted the sidewalk and approached a saloon called *The Golden Nugget* a man caught him by the arm.

"You Kelso, mister?"

"Yes."

"When're you startin' to trade?"

"Tomorrow at first light."

"Any chance tonight?"

"No."

The man grinned slyly.

"First come first served," he said. "There won't be a chance in the mornin'. I've got gold."

"Show it us tomorrow."

"I'm showin' it tonight."

It was Arch's turn to grin. "Go show it to Dawford," he suggested. The man nodded, said: "I'll do that," and walked on. Arch pushed open the door of the saloon, fought his way to the bar through a press of rangemen and miners and finally reached the bar. He drank twice, paid his reckoning, fought his way out through the press and walked on down Main. With some hard liquor under his belt, he felt up to facing Martha. At the intersection, he turned down Donovan, walked a couple of blocks and found himself in a quiet part of the town. Cottonwoods loomed dark and sinister in the moonlight here. Only a few lights showed. Here trim and neat stood Martha Dean's house surrounded by its white picket fence. He couldn't see them in the dim light, but here he knew were carefully tended flowers and shrubs. Everything Martha did was done with care. She liked things just so. Even her men and that was one reason Arch doubted she could see anything in him she could like.

Arch didn't fool himself about himself. He was wild and always had been. That is, he appeared wild to respectable women like Martha. Maybe that in itself was an attraction, but he doubted it. Martha was a strong-minded woman who had fended for herself in a tough world since she was a tender age. And she had managed to keep herself respectable and respected. It was said, and he had no reason to doubt it, that some of the biggest men in this section of Arizona had courted her at one time or another. And, he was pleased also to hear, had been sent away with fleas in their ears. That was one of the reasons for the legend that Martha didn't like men.

Arch didn't believe that. One look at Martha was enough to tell a man that she was born for the act of love and to rear fine children. At least for the right man.

He opened the picket gate, walked along the short path among the gentle scent of flowers and rapped on the door with the butt of his quirt. A few moments and the door opened an inch. An eye showed and then the door was opened wide. Arch's woman-hungry eyes took in the sight of her.

Dawford was right—Martha undoubtedly had the face of a horse. But it was a mighty handsome and wellbred horse. A woman like her didn't need a pretty face. Her hair was a glorious Titian, her figure superb: narrow in the waist, broad in the hips and full in the breasts. She held herself proudly like a dancer. Her eyes were magnificent and she radiated a character and charm that had floored better men than

Arch Kelso. And all this was wasted on a bunch of kids. She was a school-marm.

"Why, Arch Kelso," she exclaimed. Her generous mouth parted in a wide smile to reveal strong and white teeth.

"You sound surprised, Martha," Arch said. "You mean you didn't hear we was in town?"

She stepped back to allow him to enter and said: "Of course I knew you were in town, but you must allow a woman to be womanly and show an innocent surprise." She closed the door behind him and he knew that she was taking a risk, her being the only schoolteacher in town and allowing a man inside her house without a chaperon. He grinned at her and wondered how he had ever managed to keep his lusty hands off her.

"My God, Martha," he told her, "you're as beautiful as ever."

She looked annoyed. "You say that every time you see me, right off."

"I have to. Heck, you always take me by surprise. When I'm away from you I kind of picture you to myself and I picture you as beautiful as any woman can be and then when I come back and see you in the flesh, you take me by surprise again."

She put her hands on her hips.

"Are we going to spend the whole evening with you saying sweet nothings to me or are we going to talk like adult human beings?" she demanded.

"For all I care," he said, "we don't have to say a durned word. All I want to do is look at you."

"Come into the kitchen," she said, "I'm making coffee."

They went into the kitchen and he saw that there were two cups on the table.

"You expecting somebody?" he asked.

She gave him a bright look and raised his hopes as she always did when she had downed them. "You," she said.

He sank into a chair.

"We ain't talkin' all evenin'," he said. "We have just one hour."

"After which," she said, "friend Dawford will be out on the town while you watch the store."

"That's about it," he agreed.

She came near him at the table while she poured coffee. She smelled vaguely of wild flowers and new-mown hay. He looked up at her and thought she was the most appetising woman he had ever known.

When she put the coffee pot down on the table, he took her by the wrist. She didn't fight. She looked at him and said: "Now, Arch, don't start."

"I never left off. Listen, Martha, I have one hour. Tomorrow will be full of making money. I don't know how soon after that we'll pull out of town."

She smiled.

"No man ever got any place with me in a hurry."

"No man ever got any place with you, period," he told her.

"You sound angry."

"I am angry. I hate to think of a fine woman like you bein' wasted."

"Who says I'm wasted? I earn my keep. You don't mean wasted. You mean how can I resist the masculine charms of one Arch Kelso."

Arch grinned.

"I reckon that's about what I mean. Hell, Martha, don't you like me a-tall?"

She took her wrist out of his grip, sat down opposite him at the table and sipped her coffee.

She looked at him over the rim and her eyes defeated him.

"I like you fine," she said.

"What does that mean? That you an' me can talk for a few minutes every time I come into town, smile nicely and then tell each other goodbye. Martha, we ain't gettin' any younger. You gotta make hay while the sun shines."

"You won't win your case," she said, "by telling me I'm old."

He leaned forward across the table, eyeing her earnestly.

"Martha, did you ever kiss a feller?"

She got as near as a lady like her could to snorting.

"That's a stupid question. Did I ever eat a meal? Did I ever take a drink of water?"

"You're human then?"

"Did you ever think I wasn't?"

"I tried to kiss you once. You hit me so hard my ears rang tunes for a week."

"That wasn't because I didn't like being kissed. I knew ours wasn't a brief friendship and I didn't want you to think that I was easy to make."

He stood up.

"You mean you don't mind if I kiss you right now?"

She eyed him coldly.

"Don't tell me that's a cue for your masculinity to rear its ugly head," she said.

He walked around the table and stood by her. She twisted her head to look up at him. The movement stretched the fine white column of her throat. Her breasts lifted intoxicatingly.

"I have less than one hour," he said. "After that I may not see you for another six months. It's now or never. Can you sit there and tell me you don't give one solitary damn for me?"

He jumped in surprise when she reached out and took his hand in one of hers.

"I give a damn for you," she told him. "That's why I wish you weren't in town. That's why I wish you were miles away in Tucson."

"What's that supposed to mean?"

"It means you don't know this town now," she said. "This is the last wild town on the frontier. This is the last of the frontier. The last town where anything goes. The place is full of cut-throats and road-agents. Men have been killed in the last week for an ounce of gold, had their throats cut in alleyways for a nugget. What do you think's going to happen to you when you've sold your stores and made your fortune?"

He said: "You mean you're scared for me?"

"I mean I think somebody's going to try and take your money from you and while that's happening you could get killed. And I don't want that to happen."

"My God," he said, "you have feelin's after all."

The blood rushed to her face. Her grip on his hand tightened.

"You fool," she said. "Because I don't jump into bed with the first man who propositions me, do you think I don't have any feelings? Don't you know anything about women?"

He softened toward her suddenly. His anger died abruptly.

"I'm sorry," he said. "You're right. I'm a fool."

He lifted the hand in his and kissed it. She gave a little chuckle and said: "That was really gallant. I didn't know you had it in you."

He grinned.

"It was the only part of you I dared kiss."

She lifted her face and pouted her lips. He bent his head and laid his mouth on hers. Either he lifted her from her chair or she rose to meet him. He never knew. But suddenly she was in his arms and he heard heavenly music. At first, she gave him only her mouth, then slowly, her mouth opened under his and her arms stole around his neck. Lastly, her body slowly came to meet his and clung there. He felt his pulse pounding madly, his whole being seemed to be afire and the flames enveloped them both. When she drew her mouth away from his, they were both breathless and feeling shaken.

They looked into each other's eyes.

"My God," Arch said.

"Precisely," she agreed. "I knew it would be like that between us. Maybe that's why I always postponed it."

"Is there anything wrong with it being like that?" he demanded. "If it's like that, why've we wasted all this time?"

"Maybe because once that was proved, I couldn't bear for you to go away from me again." She came back into his arms and laid her head against his shoulder. He rested a cheek against her hair.

"Just this trip," he said. "Maybe a return run to Tucson. I'll have made my stake. Then we won't never be apart again."

"Could you ever settle down, Arch?"

"You bet your sweet life I could. An' will. When this Indian scare's done, I'm goin' to buy me the sweetest piece of land in this territory and build me a house on it no girl could ever resist."

"I wish I could believe that."

"I believe it."

She smiled and gave him her mouth again.

Witt Brand, who had been set to follow Arch Kelso, when Doc had spotted the tall man walking down Main, gave Arch five minutes inside Martha's house and then decided that time would stand still for the pair of them for a while. He built and lit a smoke and sauntered along to the *Golden Nugget*, where he found Doc and the boys drinking and playing poker. Doc was winning. He always won, even if he didn't have the cards because it was known to be dangerous to beat him. Only a damn fool pilgrim ever had the nerve to beat Doc and he never did it a second time. Either because he was too scared to or too dead.

Witt surveyed the table, pushed his hat onto the back of his head and as Doc looked up at him, said: "He went into his woman's house."

Doc grunted, threw in his hand and picked

up the winnings he hadn't won. There were no protests from around the table. He sat considering for a moment, wondering whether this was something he could delegate to his inferiors or if he should go and handle this personally. He had a healthy respect for Kelso and the way he could handle himself and a gun, so he decided that he had better go along to attend to this himself. He downed the remainder of his drink, thought a moment on Kelso's speed and took another drink from the bottle. He always considered he shot better when well liquored. Maybe he was right or maybe he only *thought* he was better. It was ever thus with men who lived by the gun.

He kicked the chair from under Dirk. The giant blond measured his length on the floor. His brothers laughed, but nobody else dared to. To laugh at a Brand signed a death warrant as surely as did to beat Doc at cards. Dirk picked himself up and dusted himself off. His brothers pushed back their chairs and stood.

Doc walked for the door and the rest trooped after him.

On the sidewalk, Doc stopped and said: "We'll need rifles for this." The brothers went to their horses and heaved their carbines from their saddle-boots.

Rod said: "Hell, Doc, Kelso don't have no rifle."

Doc snickered and said: "No, but we do. We ain't doin' this for fun. We ain't playin' games. We aim to have a man dead."

At the intersection of Main and Donovan, they halted as one man as they came face to face with a solitary figure standing there in the lamplight. His white linen gleamed. The butts of his twin Colt's guns were forward and high on either hip. His marshal's badge caught the lamplight.

John Stratton said: "You look like you're bent on business, men."

"Sure," said Doc, "we're goin' to kill a varmint."

The bluntness of the answer took the marshal a-back.

"Pretty big varmint for four rifles," he said.

"Biggish," Doc said. He knew that he was in a dangerous position in spite of his own speed and his being backed by four good guns. Stratton was no good, he took a rake off from every vice in town and some of the virtues as well, but he would not tolerate any usurping of

89

his own position of hired gun in town. Doc always trod lightly around him. Till now it had been a matter of live and let live on both sides. If Doc pulled a stunt it was carefully pulled outside the marshal's jurisdiction.

Stratton said: "I reckon I'm capable of killing any varmints that need it in town."

Doc said: "This one's purely poisonous, John. Five good men can just about handle him."

Stratton knew that his position at the moment was not a strong one and, though deadly with a gun, he was no hero with suicidal tendencies.

"I don't want to hear it or see it," he said. "Any trouble and I'll take action."

Doc smiled gently and managed to look like a wolverine devouring a corpse.

"There could be profit in this for us all. And a varmint out of the way," he said. "Look the other way, John, and block your ears for the next thirty minutes."

"I do have to go to the other end of town," Stratton admitted.

He nodded, pushed through them and went on his way. Doc and the Brand boys sighed with relief. Meeting the marshal had given them a nasty turn. They walked on till they came within sight of Martha Dean's house. Doc stopped and placed his men.

"Witt an' me," he said, "will shoot from the other side of the street. Dirk, get around the back. Maybe he'll sneak out that way. Stet an' Rod, get over on the left there behind that wagon. Nobody shoots till I do. Now, I want that bastard dead, hear? Mel's tough, but he ain't nothin' without Kelso around. We do this neat an' everythin' will be plain sailin' in the future."

Silently, the big men walked off to their positions.

Doc and Witt took up their positions in the shadows opposite the house. Doc found that he was sweating. He always sweated before he killed a man.

In the darkness of the hall, Arch took Martha in his arms. He knew that he was good and sunk now. The woman had him besotted. And he liked it. He felt good.

"Honey," he said, "I feel so damn good it ain't real."

She kissed him and said: "Look out for yourself, Arch. Please. I couldn't bear anything to happen now."

"I'm a coward from here on," he said. "Absolutely no trouble."

"That's my boy," she told him.

They released each other and he opened the door. He turned for a moment, as he stepped out of the doorway, to tell her: "I'll see you before we leave." He saw the flash of her smile.

He took two paces away from the house.

A rifle slammed flatly.

Something stung him like a red-hot poker on his left shoulder. Several other reports followed so closely on each other that they were one continuous sound. A window collapsed with a crash of glass. He turned and hurled himself back the way he had come, crashing the half-open door back and bowling Martha violently from her feet. They both landed full length on the hall floor. He twisted and kicked the door shut with a heel. It slammed noisily and there was a sudden deathly silence in the house for a brief moment.

"My God," Martha said.

"Upstairs," Arch hissed.

She scrambled to her knees in the darkness and reached out for him.

"Arch," she said.

"Get upstairs." He pushed her away from

him. They scrambled to their feet and she clung to him.

"They tried to kill you."

"They weren't throwin' me kisses."

"What will you do?"

"Get out of here."

"You can't. Stay inside. You'll be safe here."

He took her in a strong grip on either arm. He sounded angry when he spoke.

"You get upstairs, girl. I know what I'm doin'. I have to move fast."

She was as angry as he.

"You're not going out there. I will not have you killed. Stay here and don't be a fool."

"I'll be a rat in a trap here. I have to go." All the while, his ears were cocked for sounds from outside.

"You're thinking of me," she said. "Don't. Stay here and stay alive."

"You bet your sweet life I'm thinkin' of you. I'm thinkin' of me too. Now quit yammering an' get up them stairs." He took hold of her bodily and got her to the stairs, pushing her up them and shouting at her to do as she was told. The urgency of his voice moved her and she went.

As soon as the sound of her movements had

ceased, he stood still for a moment, listening. He could hear nothing. Time had passed since the firing of the shots and the men out front had had time to change their positions. He knew that more than one man had made a try for him. That meant it wasn't going to be easy to get out of this one. They had rifles and he had only his Remington ·44. His only chance was to slip away under cover of the dark. That meant the rear. But he'd bet there was at least one man waiting for him there. But whatever happened, he must get them away from the house and Martha. The chances were that they meant her no harm. He wondered who the hell they were. He ticked off the names of the men who hated him enough to kill him and knew that knowing the names of the men wouldn't help at all.

He moved through the house, feeling his way with his left hand, reached the kitchen and then the rear door. He felt for the bolts and drew them back. He was tempted for one weak moment to stay in the comparative safety of the house and then, ashamed, he braced himself to open the door a fraction. He lifted the Remington from leather and took a deep breath.

Wrenching the door wide, he drove out into

the blackness of the night, struck dirt with his right shoulder, somersaulted and came to his feet, ran two rapid paces and flung himself flat. Only then did it seem that the shot came. He heard it crash into the kitchen and knew that at least one marksman was off to his right. There was timber there and the blackness beneath the trees was complete.

He lay still, regaining his breath.

Feet pounded along the side of the house and a man shouted: "You get him, Dirk?"

The street light silhouetted the man.

Arch raised the Remington, took careful aim and fired.

The shot spun the man around and he fell against the side of the house.

"Christ," he called. "Aw, Christ . . . he's killed me."

Arch crawled toward the timber for a half-dozen yards and lay still again, ears and eyes sharp. The whole town seemed to have gone silent.

He started to crawl again until he reached Martha's picket fence. This presented a problem. He could so easily give himself away getting over it. He wondered what Martha was thinking back in the house there. One thing he was more or less certain of: the man he had shot had called the name Dirk. That pointed to the Brand brothers. That meant he was up against at least four of them. And maybe Doc Dooley was along too. If so that meant real trouble and he would be lucky to get out of this alive.

He began to work his way along the fence to the left, feeling for the gate. His left shoulder was burning now. It was not too painful, but it was irksome. He wondered if he showed in the gloom against the white of the fence.

He reached the gate, put up his left hand and lifted the latch. The gate swung in toward him and he crawled through. He was now on a rough dirt path. He started along it to the right so that he was headed for the man in the timber. If he could down that one he knew he would be clear in that direction.

A snapping click reached his ears and he knew that a man had levered a fresh round into the breach of a rifle. Another sound followed—the soft music of spurs. A man was walking toward him, treading softly.

Arch bunched his legs under him and heard the sound of his teeth grinding together.

In a moment, the dark dim form of a man

loomed against the faint light of the sky. Arch launched himself, driving his right shoulder hard into the belly of the man who gave out a massive sigh as the wind was knocked out of him. They went down in a heap with Arch at once astride the man and slashing at him savagely with the barrel of the Remington. Once he struck flesh and drove a yell of pain from the man beneath him; once he struck the hat-covered skull. The form beneath him went still.

Arch got up, holstered the Remington and groped around till he found the fallen rifle. Quickly, he went through the man's pockets till he had found some spare cartridges. Transferring these to his own pocket, he stood and listened. Brush crackled ahead of him. Somebody was pounding across Martha's back yard. He heard them reach the gate and, slamming the butt of the rifle into his shoulder, he fired and levered, fired and levered. A yell of alarm came.

The man in the timber opened up and the man in the yard shouted with alarm again. Arch cut across to his left to outflank the man under the trees, ran a dozen yards and dropped flat.

So far so good. The Brand boys had suffered

a fifty per cent casualty. They had learned it wasn't easy to tangle with a Kelso.

He Indianed forward, using elbows and toes, eyes on the dark of the trees. The man there fired. The shot didn't come near Arch, showing that the man had no idea where he was.

Arch waited.

A sound behind him.

The man in Martha's back yard was coming out and pussyfooting toward him.

A sound ahead.

The man ahead was coming out of the trees. If they both kept on going, they could both meet up right where Arch was lying. He felt around for a stone and succeeded in finding a can. He picked this up and hurled it away to his right. Nothing happened. Both pairs of footsteps came on.

He started to move off to the left.

At once, a voice behind him, bellowed: "There he goes."

A shot sounded and something tore up the dirt right in his face. He rolled desperately to the right, came to his knees and fired and levered as fast as he knew how at an uncertain form that showed between himself and the house. The man from the timber started to fire.

The rifle in Arch's hands clicked harmlessly and he hurled it away from him, snapping his right hand down on the Remington and tearing it from leather.

From further off a man howled: "Kill him. Kill him, hear?"

He knew that was Doc Dooley.

A bullet ripped at the sleeve of his shirt.

There was nothing left for him to do but the insanest thing of all. Turning and yelling like a Comanche, he made a mad dash at the man coming from timber. Once he tripped on some trash and nearly went down. Every second of that crazy charge, he expected lead to pound into his flesh either from the front or rear. But he must have taken both men unawares. The shooting stopped and before he knew what was happening there, slightly to his right, was the dark form of a man. There was no more than time to swerve in that direction, cock the Remington and fire once and then he was into the man.

They made sounds like two bull buffaloes coming together. They were both big men and heavy. The other man staggered back a pace and must have swung up the butt of his rifle because something very heavy struck Arch under his ribcage. It hurt and it stopped him. The whole front of him seemed to explode in pain. In the second of motionless silence that followed he heard the other man pounding forward. He made a back-handed slash with his pistol and missed. The man brought the butt of his rifle down, Arch tried to dodge and received the blow on his right shoulder. This drove him to one knee.

He heard the giant intake of breath as the man swung the weapon for a lethal blow. Tilting the Remington, he fired almost point-blank. The heavy ball tore the man from his feet and dumped him on the ground. Arch staggered to his feet, turned and pointed the Remington at the other man who was now looming out of the murk. The only response he got from the pressure on the trigger was an empty click.

Panic swept over him.

Flight was the only thing that could save him now, and he reckoned it was too late for that. However, he turned and lunged toward the trees.

At once his foot caught in something on the ground and he went headlong. He knew that he had fallen over the man he had shot. He went one way and his gun the other. In the scrambling haste of utter fear, he got to his feet and ran. Two shots came from behind and hummed past him, adding speed to his already racing legs. It seemed that he ran for an age before he was in the merciful darkness of the trees. He ran into a trunk in his path and nearly knocked himself out, but he ploughed on, not stopping till he had come to the bank of the creek. Here he fell in complete exhaustion and lay full-length, panting and gasping air into his tortured lungs. Then he listened and heard no sound but that of the water. He crawled to it and drank deep.

When he had regained his breath, he waded through the water and slowly clambered up the bank to the other side. There was time then to think of Martha and her back there wondering if he was alive or dead.

7

HE saw the camp long before he reached it. Flare torches and fires cut into the darkness of the night. And in the flickering light from the flames he saw the queue of people and heard Mel bellowing for order and that he had only one pair of hands. Inside the circle of wagons, he saw their men straining at heavy loads.

He had to grin. Mel wasn't going to have his night on the town after all.

He tramped wearily around the rear of the wagons away from the townspeople and entered the circle.

When Mel caught sight of him, he bellowed: "Where the hell you been? Never here when I need you."

"I've been bushwhacked," Arch told him.

Mel took a poke of gold from a man over a rough counter of a plank across two barrelheads and heaved a large sack of flour to him. He turned and snarled at Arch: "What you think I've been? Don't you call this bein' bushwhacked? Here, take over. Nobody ain't doin' me outa my night on the town. If I don't have a drink an' a woman mighty soon I'm goin' to break out in boils."

Arch had had enough.

"You can go to hell far as I care," he said.

Mel laughed, stooped under the rough counter and swaggered off into the night. Charlie Garth came up and said: "What happened to you, Arch?"

Arch said: "There ain't time now. Tell you later." A man at the counter was bellowing for nails and banging the plank with a clenched fist. "How about Ben Goodall?"

"The doc came out from town and patched him up. Ben's in town gettin' drunk."

"Do you have nails or don't you?"

"Nails comin' up," Charlie' sang out and hefted a keg. He and the man started to haggle about the price. A woman pushed forward and demanded flour.

They didn't stop all night. Tirelessly it seemed the people came, paying mostly in gold dust and nuggets for the benefits of civilisation that had been denied them for so long. It was a sellers market and Arch and Charlie saw to it that the sellers didn't lose out. By dawn, every man in the crew was ready to drop. Mel staggered back from town looking like a drained shadow of a man, crept under a wagon and fell asleep. By then every wagon load had been sold, except for the few supplies that Arch and Mel needed to retain. Arch got rid of the crowd with some difficulty, hitched a team to a wagon and with Charlie toting a shot-gun and with two other armed men along, he went into town to the bank and got out an irate bank owner to put their winnings in a safe place. The four of them then took a drink in the nearest saloon, drove back to camp and got into their blankets.

It was only then that Arch thought of Martha. He called himself all the meanest names he could think of, threw aside the blanket, heaved on his boots, hitched his gunbelt and walked into town.

He was too tired to be wary. He told himself that it was daylight and that even Doc Dooley wouldn't be stupid enough to try anything in daylight, but he wasn't fully convinced. His right hand was never far from his gun.

He met John Stratton on Main, clean-shaven, his long hair combed and immaculate, his boots brightly polished. He felt like something the coyote rejected in comparison. He was dirty, unshaven and bleary-eyed.

Stratton grinned and said: "Anybody tell you you look awful, Arch?"

"Most everybody," Arch said and walked on, not being in the mood for Stratton right then. Over his shoulder, he said: "You wasn't marshalling so good last night, Johnny."

Stratton stared after him frowning.

When he reached Martha's house, he wondered if she would be teaching in school. Then he heard a church-bell ring and he reckoned it was Sunday and she would be home, maybe preparing for church. He rapped on her white door with his knuckles, waited a few minutes and pounded with his fist.

The door opened and Martha stood there in crisp gingham looking good enough to eat.

"Just thought I'd let you know I was still alive." he said.

Her eyes snapped and his heart sank. She was mad. And he knew she had a right to be mad.

"You just thought to come and tell me that?" she said. "Why, you no-good, thoughtless—"

"I been busy," he said lamely.

"Too busy to let me know if you were alive or dead?"

"Well, I—"

"Come inside."

"It's broad daylight. Maybe people'll talk."

"Come inside and quit yammering."

He stepped into the house and she slammed the door. Suddenly, she was in his arms and her face was buried in his neck and he had the feeling she was crying.

"What the hell—?" he said.

She leaned back in his arms and he saw that there were tears in her eyes.

"You big ape," she said. "You great lummiking fool. Do you think I didn't know you were alive. I came out to your camp and made sure. You think I'd be here quietly getting ready for church not knowing if you were alive or dead?"

He clasped her to him and tried to kiss her, but she tore herself loose from him.

"You stink of whiskey and sweat," she cried. "Get those filthy clothes off and take a bath."

"All I want is sleep. We've been tradin' all night."

"You can sleep when you're clean." She led the way into the kitchen and started filling pots and pans with water and putting them on the stove. He sank wearily down on a chair. She

106

put wood on the stove and thrust a cup of coffee in front of him. He drank and it tasted wonderful. She threw off her bonnet and brought a bath in from an outhouse. He fell asleep over the table and only woke when she shook him vigorously.

"Wake up, get up and wash up," she said.

He opened his eyes and saw the steaming bath. It looked inviting, but he would rather have slept.

"Get out," he said, "an' I'll make a start."

"You're overly modest," she told him. "I've seen a man before. I had five brothers and I always washed their backs."

"You ain't washing no back of mine."

Five minutes later covered in confusion and soap suds, he was in the bath and she was scrubbing his back. It seemed to make her happy. He had to admit that the bath made him feel good. When he had done washing, he modestly draped a big towel around himself and dried off. He looked around for his clothes and couldn't find them.

"What did you do with my clothes?" he asked.

Solemnly, she said: "I hid them. There's a bed upstairs. Get up there an' sleep in it."

"I have to get back to camp."

"Why?"

"There's things to do."

"You'll go back and sleep."

"Maybe."

"Then sleep here. It must be over a week since you slept in a comfortable bed."

"You're tempting me. You have to think of the neighbours."

"I don't give one solitary Yankee damn for the neighbours."

He sighed.

"An' I thought," he said, "you was a modest, shy, conventional woman."

She put her hands on her hips. Her hair had come loose in the steam and she was flushed in the heat. She looked mighty beautiful.

"Maybe you know horses and maybe you know men," she said with her head on one side and a faint smile on her lips, "but, boy, you don't know the first thing about women."

"I'm beginning to see that. Get out of my way and let me get to that bed."

She stepped out of the way and bowed him to the door.

"Ham and eggs when you wake," she told him.

108

He stopped and grinned at her.

"You're trying to break down my resistance," he accused her.

"Bullseye," she confirmed. She blew him a kiss and he padded on naked feet down the hall, up the stairs and found that the only bed in the house was in her room. It was a great many years since he had last been into a room belonging to a woman and it took him back a mite. He stood hesitating in the doorway, feeling he shouldn't be there. But the white linen of the bed invited him and he weakened. The place smelled headily of woman. Her personal things lay on the table by the window: brushes, combs, a ribbon or two. He stepped into the room, dropped the towel on the floor and got into bed. The sheets were refreshingly cool. He stretched in sheer luxury and found himself to be a man he had forgotten. He thought for a moment of Martha and imagined her lying in bed here with him. The thought was very pleasant. And then he fell into a deep sleep.

He awoke once to find that the curtains had been drawn across the window. The room was dim and quiet, the sound of the town a long way off. Slowly and deliciously, he sank back into sleep again.

When he finally woke, the sun was going down and it was dusk in the room. He reached out a hand and found flesh. Startled, he opened his eyes and saw Martha's head on the pillow next to his.

"My God," he exclaimed and sat up in bed in alarm. The movement revealed the upper part of the woman's body. The sight of it stilled him and he looked at it in wonder. Her eyes were closed, but he knew that she wasn't asleep.

"Martha," he said, "this is a Goddam trap." She opened her eyes lazily and rolled over onto her back.

"We're both caught, I guess," she said. She reached out a hand and pulled him down beside her. She didn't have to pull very hard. Their arms went around each other and he kissed her hair. It smelled of sunshine and sun-kissed wheat.

"The neighbours know I'm here," he said. "You'll never be able to look them in the eyes again."

"I never knew a man so worried about the neighbours," she said. "They know you're here, they know I'm here. They're talking already. But it doesn't matter. We'll go to the judge in the morning."

He started.

"What's that?" he demanded.

"You don't think," she said, "I'd make love with you today, if we weren't going to be married in the morning. After all I'm a modest, shy, conventional woman."

He laughed outright. He had never known a woman like her and was never likely to.

"You take the biscuit, honey. Say, how about that ham and eggs?"

"First things first," she told him and pulled him close. He clean forgot about the ham and eggs. He forgot about everything, including the neighbours and the judge in the morning and was conscious only of the woman in the bed with him.

8

DOC DOOLEY was mad. He couldn't remember when he had been madder. He sat in the big bedroom shared by the Brand brothers, he drank and he offered them a furious tirade that they couldn't refuse. Two of them lay in their beds feeling awful. Stet had had the flesh torn off a couple of ribs by a heavy forty-four bullet. Both ribs felt as though they had been shattered. The doctor from down the street said they were okay but Stet didn't believe him. Rod lay next to him feeling that he had been kicked repeatedly by a Kentucky mule on the top of his thick skull. He hadn't. He had been hit over the head with the long barrel of a Remington ·44 revolver. At home in the tender care of his wife lay Dirk who had had his temple grazed none too gently by a round from that self-same Remington. Witt sat on the edge of the bed showing no hurt except to his pride. The brothers had singly or together been lawmen or outlaws in every state and territory west of the Missouri. They had swaggered, shot and buffaloed their way out of and into any situation they wished. And now they had been suckered by one single solitary man. The pain it gave them was as sharp as a knife.

Doc was saying: "One man. One solitary man on his Goddam lonesome with an itsy-bitsy little pistol. Four great hulking swaggering, gun-proud, husky, tough, randy, fightin', rootin', tootin' fightin' men was kicked around by that same pulin' hick of a cow-nurse and made to look like sonsabitchin' schoolteachers. Christ, you oughta be cryin' your eyes out like little whipped kids."

Witt said: "You was there."

Doc snarled: "Don't you give me no lip or I'll ram them pearly teeth down your lily-white throat."

Witt glowered. That was all he dared do.

Doc started off again, taking a drink of whiskey every time he paused to take breath. He went on for a long time till Witt groaned and said: "Talk ain't goin' to get us no place. We have to decide what we have to do."

"*I'll* decide what we have to do. I've decided already. You Goddam sweety-boys have to get yourself all healed up so we can go after Kelso and Dawford and settle their hash. The dust they picked up from trading'd keep us comfortable for a couple of years alone. But there's goin' to be more. There's goin' to be more gold than you or me ever dreamt of. Ringus come to me with talk. A half-dozen mine owners, the big boys, went to Dawford and propositioned him. It's gotta be Dawford an' Kelso're goin' tote a whole heap of gold outa here. An' I'm tellin' you right here an' now, that gold ain't goin' to reach Tucson. It's goin' to disappear into thin air on the trail an' it's goin' to disappear into our pockets, boys."

Witt said: "Hell, the boys is hurt bad."

"Hurt bad my ass," Doc shouted. "I marched for a month with worse hurts than they got all put together during the war. When the time comes, they're goin' to forget all this damned nonsense; they're goin' to get outa that bed and they're goin' to get into the saddle and ride."

Stet moaned.

"I couldn't ride a hobby horse," he said.

Doc stood up.

"You make me puke," he said, picked up his bottle and strode out of the room. As he reached the bottom of the stairs, Ringus came into the house through the kitchen.

"What news, Ringus, my son?" Doc asked.

Ringus was eager.

"It's all over town, Doc," he said. "Kelso an' Dawford is definitely carryin' out the gold."

"When?" Doc demanded.

"I don't know."

Doc clenched his fists and waved them at the ceiling.

"God preserve me from clowns," he said. "Get out into town, take a drink here an' there and open your ears. I want to know when they're goin' an' how many men they'll have with them."

"I can't drink without cash," Ringus said looking half-pathetic and half smart.

Doc sighed gently, took a coin from his pocket and tossed it to the other. Ringus disappeared with great rapidity.

Doc took a drink from the bottle. He went into his shabby parlor and looked at the street. He liked to watch the passing people and to think. He knew that his big chance was right in his lap. He would make his stake, shuck the Brand boys and go to San Francisco and live in style. He'd eat of the best, have a great mansion

115

choked to the eaves with the most expensive furniture, a cabinet full of the best drink, pretty maids who would do anything for the master, a box at the opera, carriage and blood horses so that men and women would turn their heads and say: "There goes the famous Doctor Dooley." Or maybe he'd change his name. Make a fresh start. The idea appealed to him.

A tall figure walking in the dust of the street caught his eye. Arch Kelso. Doc stared malignantly, hating. Any man who beat him at any stage of the game, he hated. He experienced an impulse to speak to the man. Quickly he went out of the room, trotted through the hall and went out onto the street as Kelso came by.

"Kelso."

The tall man stopped, staring somberly at the ungainly figure before him.

"What can I do for you, Doc?"

"Nothin'. Just wondered how you was keepin'. You 'n' Dawford. My old friend."

"We're doin' all right. I heard you wasn't doin' too good yourself."

Doc spread his thick hands.

"Sometimes the cards fall for you, sometimes they don't. My luck'll turn."

Kelso grinned faintly.

"You an' the Brand boys'll have to shoot a mite straighter in future if you want that to happen," he said.

Doc started. He hadn't been aware that Kelso knew of the identity of his attackers.

"You want to be careful what you say, boy," he said.

Kelso came up to him, looked down at him from his height and prodded him in his massive chest with a hard forefinger.

"You come for me or Mel again," he said, "an' you're liable to get yourself killed, Doc."

Doc fell back a pace, looking shocked.

"What kinda talk is this?" he demanded. "My word, Kelso, are you threatening me?"

"Yeah," Arch said.

A voice said: "Did I hear the word 'threat', boys?" They turned their heads and saw John Stratton standing there in his glory.

Before Doc could say a word, Arch said: "You surely did, Johnny. I was threatening Doc if he ever tried to bushwhack me again I'd be liable to kill him."

"If Doc objects to that kind of talk and wants to make a charge," Stratton said, "I could run you in for that, Arch."

Arch smiled unpleasantly.

117

"Go ahead, Doc," he said. "Object away. I'm in a rare mood for trouble."

"Hello, Arch, dear. I'm ready."

Martha appeared on the scene. Doc stared at her loveliness hungrily out of his little pig's eyes. Stratton regarded her coldly. He always liked to be the most beautiful thing in sight.

"Why, Martha," Arch said, "you just spoiled these boys' fun."

She looked from one to the other.

"Why?"

"Doc was twittin' me it wasn't him an' the Brand boys tried to kill me the other night. An' Johnny there was saying if I accused Doc of it he could run me in. You see, they're both fast with a gun, but they ain't quite sure if they're faster'n me. Johnny would of drawn on me years back, but he never could quite get up the nerve. Doc, here, prefers to shoot in the dark. They're both a mite yaller in their own ways."

Stratton went white. His rage was ice cold.

Doc was the opposite. He seethed with boiling hot fury.

Stratton said: "Real brave of you, Arch, with a woman around."

Doc was so enraged that he couldn't speak.

Arch said: "Walk on down to the judge's place, Martha."

She turned on him.

"If you think I'm going to let you brawl on my wedding day, you're mistaken."

Arch snapped: "Get goin', Martha."

Doc found his voice.

"There's liable to be a funeral instead of a weddin'."

Martha said: "When I walk down the street, you come with me."

Arch raised his voice a little.

"Martha," he said, "you don't walk ahead, there's goin' to be no weddin'."

She stared at him for a moment in silence, then abruptly turned on her heel and marched across the street. She only went as far as the sidewalk. There she stopped and watched the three men. Anger went from her eyes and fear took its place.

Arch turned to Stratton and Doc Dooley.

"You're in good company, Johnny," he said. "You pair up pretty good with a little cut-throat like Doc."

Doc's right hand jerked involuntarily.

Stratton cleared his throat.

"Arch," he said, "I'm goin' to get you before

you leave town. You stepped off on the wrong foot when I rode out to meet you. This is my town an' don't you forget it."

Doc looked amazed. He knew that Stratton was backing down for now.

"You heard this man threaten me, marshal," he said.

Stratton said: "That means you can defend yourself." He smiled faintly. "I've been a witness to the whole scene."

Doc knew that he had been given a clean sheet to kill Arch Kelso. Every muscle in his thick body braced itself for the fatal move. But his brain didn't send the message to act. He knew the risk was too great.

A man's voice that cut in on the scene decided him.

"Having trouble, Arch?"

They all turned and saw Mel Dawford standing on the nearest sidewalk. There was a double-barreled greener in his hands.

Arch said: "No trouble a-tall, Mel."

Mel said: "That's funny, for a moment I thought I'd have to shoot a yaller-bellied polecat or two."

Stratton and Doc knew the moment was well passed now. They would both have to wait. But they did not move, not even away, with that shot-gun looking at them.

Mel said: "Move along, boys. Me an' Mr. Kelso have private matters to talk over."

Doc walked off into his house without a backward glance.

Stratton said: "This ain't finished, Arch," and turned on his heel. Straight-backed he strode down the street. Mel stepped down into the dust.

"For Crissake," he said, "where've you been?"

"Visitin'."

Martha stepped down from the sidewalk and came toward them. Mel looked at her wide-eyed.

"Aw, no," he said. "Not with Martha." He caught Arch by the arm. "Come on, boy. You'n me have to meet the mine owners. They've made us a good proposition."

"Later," Arch told him.

Martha came up and Mel said: "Good mornin', Martha," to her. She gave him a cool reply. Mel said: "There ain't no later, Arch. This is business. The owners're at the Imperial right now, waitin' on us."

"Later," Martha said. "Right now, we're getting married."

Mel's jaw fell open wide.

"Aw, no," he exclaimed as if the end of the world had come.

"Oh, yes," declared Martha.

They argued about it. Mel seemed to think that if he shouted loud enough and stamped around a bit, he could persuade Martha and Arch to change their minds. After five minutes or so, he seemed to realise that he wasn't getting anywhere, so he decided to go along, stand witness for them and wish them well. But he did it with a gloomy face as if his best friend was taking a fateful and maybe fatal step. The judge, almost sober out of respect for the early hour of the day and the ceremony he had to perform, galloped through the necessary ritual and had them hitched in about five minutes flat. He kissed the bride, Arch kissed the bride, Mel wiped his mouth with the back of his hand and kissed the bride. They then walked out into the sunshine with Martha beaming on Arch's left arm and went to the nearest restaurant for breakfast. This was Mel's second, but he put away enough food for two men.

When they had done eating, they deposited

Martha at her house and went along to the Imperial where they found a dozen mine owners gathered. They had all been drinking to kill time while they waited for the two partners. Colonel Peabody, a white-haired Virginian was their spokesman, and he got down to cases straight off.

They had, he said bluntly, one hundred thousand dollars worth of gold and they were getting their asses burned sitting on it. They wanted it out of here and in Tucson as fast as it could be managed. Had Kelso and Dawford the facilities for removing it and could they do it safely? That much money was an emperor's ransom and there wasn't a desperado in the country who wouldn't like to get his hands on it.

Arch took a drink and replied. He had his answer ready, for he and Mel had talked over the possibility of this proposition closely.

First, he said, they had to get the gold safely into one place ready for shipment. That would be the responsibility of the mine owners. Second, they must have a safe place to hold the gold before they moved out with it. He and Mel proposed that they move their camp away from the town right out onto the plain. There all approaches to the camp could be easily

123

watched. The gold must not be brought to them until they were almost ready to move out. Before they did so, all the wagons must be reinforced to carry the extra weight and, if possible, more men recruited as guards. This would not be easy, for they had to be careful of the men they hired. Only men they knew personally would fit the bill.

The colonel said, "We'll start movin' the gold a week from now. Will that give you enough time to get prepared?"

Mel said "yes", that would be ample time. There were smiths in town with idle hands. They would hire as many as they could to get the job of reinforcing the wagons done in time.

They then started to haggle about the price. This lasted an hour. It was the case of another sellers' market. The miners wanted to move their gold and there was nobody else to do it but Kelso and Dawford.

Arch and Mel walked out of the meeting happy men. They took a brief drink at the *Golden Nugget* and walked back to camp where they gave orders for camp to be struck, the wagons to be loaded and the teams hitched up.

Charlie Garth started shouting his head off. Men came running. The rumor about the gold had been in the air and they knew this move meant something. If the teams were being hitched that meant the partners had made a deal. No deal, they would have sold the wagons off. They snapped into it, caught up the mules in the rope corral and started sorting out the teams. Bedrolls were thrown into the backs of wagons, dust rolled, fires were extinguished and men shouted to Arch and Mel to know what was afoot. Mel bellowed back that they would know in good time. When the wagons were ready to move out, Arch mounted his horse and Mel went back into town to hire the blacksmiths. The train got on the move and several people came to the outskirts of town to see what was going on.

A mile from town on the edge of the creek, so there would be water for the animals, Arch consulted with Charlie Garth and they both agreed that the spot was as good as any. The wagons were laagered. The cook started to prepare the midday meal with a couple of men to gather fuel for him. There was a fair amount of brush along the banks of the creek. This Arch had cut back by the rest of the crew because it would provide cover for anybody wanting to get near the train. The job was not finished by the noon meal when the men knocked off to eat. Mel arrived from town with five blacksmiths. Arch reckoned he must have used threats as well as bribes because there were only five in the whole town. These men ate a meal and got to work with the metal they had brought out from town in a wagon. Soon after eating, the men were making music with their hammers on anvils while Arch and his crew continued with their work on the brush by the creek. Mel was for piling the cut brush under and between the wagons to prevent anybody crawling through into the laager under cover of dark, but Arch and Charlie were against that. It could be too easily fired. The wagons were dry and would burn like tinder.

When they saw the blacksmiths at work on the wagons, the men's curiosity was too much for them. Ben Goodall, his arm still in a sling, but otherwise looking all right, came to Arch and demanded to know what the hell was afoot.

"Is it true," he demanded, "you aim to tote gold into Tucson?"

Arch told him: "Does it matter, Ben, what we're totin'. You're the best man we know and you're hired."

Ben grinned.

126

"If we're goin' back through Indian country and I can knock some of the varmints off, I'm your man."

That evening when the moon was up the men sat around by firelight, that is the men who hadn't taken the chance to go into town. Mel had loaned them horses and mules to ride in and spend some money. Mel and Arch talked to the rest of the men, telling them that they aimed to make the return trip to Tucson and all of them if they wanted could come along. They were paying sixty dollars a man. That interested them. They all reckoned they'd come along. Several had families in Tucson and wanted to rejoin them and the means of making money with the Indian scare on was scarce.

That evening, Mel and Arch went into town to recruit some more men. They both thought that the colonel had been right and it was very possible that they had not only to fear Apaches on their return trip, but thieves of a different color. This was the last wild corner of the West and the territory was choked with desperadoes who had lived violently for years in various towns on the frontier. Some lawmen were good, but those that were were scattered thinly over a vast country. All there was of the law in this neck of the woods was a drunken judge and Stratton who was no better than a bandit who made his living buffaloing drunks and playing a crooked game of cards. It was also said openly in town that he took a rake-off from the red-light district of Crewsville and ruled the madames with terror. If Arch and Mel were to get the gold safely to Tucson they would have to do it with the loyalest guns they could buy.

In one saloon, they met a drunken cowhand whose only claim to distinction apparently was that he had the top of his ear missing, a knife scar down one cheek and the tally finger missing from his right hand. This was Tone Walsh. He had ridden for Arch for three years. He was the lousiest shot with a pistol a man could be, but he handled a rifle proficiently. He was good with horses, cattle and little children. He would die for the man who hired him. Sixty dollars would be a fortune to him and he would drink it or lose it at cards within a day of reaching his destination. They hired him on the spot, carried him out of the saloon because his legs wouldn't hold him, put him in the saddle of his horse and set him off in the direction of the camp.

Next they found Black Jack Owen. He was

called Black because he was black. He was an old Negro. Both Arch and Mel had known him back in Texas as boys. He had seemed old then and hadn't altered one iota since. He was still tough as whang-leather, upright and alert. He was the finest horseman they knew. He was a man who lived through his hands—a great one for braiding quirts, ropes and suchlike. Men reckoned that he could talk to horses so that the creatures understood him. He was a great hand for the wild country and could track, so both Arch and Mel would swear, a barefooted man over rock. No animal or man had ever scared him. He was an old friend and would have gone with them if they hadn't offered him money. After they had spoken with him and told him where the wagons were, he simply nodded, being a man of few words, walked to his horse, tightened the cinches and rode out of town. They combed the town for another hour, but they didn't find anybody else they could trust, so they went and begged Martha for supper, got it and settled down for a domesticated hour with her. After that she and Arch drove Mel away and she and Arch went up to bed. Arch reckoned he had had a fine day.

Before he went to sleep that night, Arch told her: "Can't do this after the gold's in camp."

She said: "Fix us a bed in a wagon. I'm coming out to join you."

"You're what?" he demanded, raising himself on one elbow.

Tersely, she told him: "You'll have to get used to having a wife along, now you're married. Where you go, I go."

"You're crazy," he said. "You can't come out there into the desert. Good grief, I'll have enough on my mind without having to worry about you."

She kissed him with a jolly laugh.

"You don't know yet what you've taken on, Arch Kelso," she informed him. "I'm a determined woman."

"I knew that before I married you. Just like you knew I'm a determined man. You don't come on no trip with me." The warmth of her body was getting through to him and his mind wasn't too much on what he was saying. "Martha, this ain't no ordinary trip. There's Indians out there and if the white bandidoes don't have a try at us my name ain't Kelso."

"That makes me all the more determined to

come along." She put her arms around his neck. "Kiss me, darling."

He kissed her and whispered: "I don't want nothin' to happen to you, Martha. Be a good girl and stay put."

"I don't have to be a good girl; just a good wife. Good wives stick with their husbands. You can waste time and talk all night, but I'm coming."

"You ain't an' that's final."

9

THEY rode out the following morning, Arch on his bay and Martha on her little roan mare. Mel nearly had a fit when he caught sight of Martha swinging down coolly from the saddle. The men all stood around and stared. Arch stood by looking bemused.

"Hello, Mel," Martha said, smiling happily.

"I hope you're here visitin', Martha," Mel said.

"No," she told him. "I'm here for the trip." Mel blew up.

"You ain't here for no trip, not while I have any say in the running of this outfit."

"You want every man you can spare for guard duty and you know it. I'll cook. I'll bet these men can do with some decent home cooking."

The men grinned, shuffled their feet and said: "You bet." Mel glared at them as if they were all traitors.

He said: "It's bad enough to makin' Arch

soft in the head. I ain't havin' that happen to the rest of my men."

"You're wasting your breath," Martha told him. One of the men rushed forward at a glance from her fine eyes to take her horse.

Mel shouted: "Don't you unsaddle that horse."

Everything happened for a while as if Mel hadn't been there. He raved impotently. Martha rolled up her sleeves and drove the cook away from the fire. He was a man who had been hired for his proficiency with mules and a rifle. He was only too pleased to give way to her. By the time the men had eaten the first of Martha's meals they voted they had never tasted a meal like it and that if Martha didn't go along, they didn't either. Mel glowered and enjoyed his meal. Mel pitched a tent for Martha and rigged up some kind of a bed for her when he had done eating.

"If you gotta come," he said, "you gotta come. Only the men ain't here to guard you from danger, ma'am. They're here to guard the gold. Just you remember that."

Martha serenely smiled and thanked him prettily. The men volunteered to wash the dishes for her, they scrambled to gather firewood. One of them rigged up a wash-basin on sticks for her and put a screen of tarps around it so she could have some privacy. Arch smoked his pipe and thought maybe it wan't such a bad thing to have a woman around a camp of men. It certainly improved their manners.

Early in the afternoon, the first consignment of gold arrived. With it came the mine owner, one Jepson Carson, with six armed men. It came in iron-bound boxes and was dumped right in the center of the camp where everybody could see it. Arch checked it into his inventory and signed for it. Carson departed leaving two of his men with the gold. Within an hour of his departure, the colonel's men arrived. Four of them this time, with a wagon heavy with gold. This was checked and signed for the same as the other and piled with it in the center of the circle of wagons. Arch and Mel now posted their guards for the coming of dusk, two of them on the far side of the creek, two on the other side of the laager and one inside the circle on the move. Two men were stationed right on the gold itself. They were taking no chances.

There were no more deliveries of gold that day, but after dark a man rode out to the camp with word that the partners should stand by for deliveries of gold from then on. That night Arch and Mel were roused cursing from their beds in the early hours as six wagons arrived from town laden with gold and in the care of a dozen men armed to the teeth with rifles and revolvers. It took the rest of the night to unload the gold and check it in. Martha got up early and cheerily prepared breakfast. As the men finished work there was hot food and drink ready for them. The wagons from the mines departed, leaving another three armed men behind. Half the little company now got into their blankets for a few hours hard-earned sleep. Arch took Mel aside.

"When do we aim to pull out?" he asked. "We have all the gold now."

"Don't let's make up our minds now," Mel said. "Let's even surprise ourselves."

Arch thought that a good idea. He sat down with a rifle across his knees and with his back to the gold and fell into a doze.

They made no move till the following day when they both agreed that it looked as if the weather would shortly change. If it rained, it could be tricky out on the desert when every arroyo could briefly become the bed of a flooding stream. They loaded the gold, scattering it throughout every wagon and adding food and water so that each wagon were a self-contained unit. There were six wagons and enough for three men to a wagon with a few left over. That would allow both Mel and Arch to ride free, which was a great help. The blacksmiths had done a good job and each wagon was now a powerfully reinforced vehicle able to tackle rough country with a heavy load on. But they were heavy and both partners had thought it wise to bring extra mules out from town. They were cheap to buy, for the animals had been eating their heads off in a feed-starved community. If Arch and Mel hadn't come along no doubt they would have soon been killed for meat. So now they had eight mules to each wagon and a dozen or so spare. This might sound like extravagance, but neither Mel nor Arch wanted the train slowed through loss of animals.

Mel went into town to buy extra arms and ammunition and managed to purchase enough shot-guns so that there were almost enough for one per wagon for close up work. He and Arch reckoned that with honest tough men and those guns they could take on an army of cut-throats, but both prayed that the necessity would not arise. Neither were happy about Martha coming along, but her determination was too much for them and they assigned her a wagon in the center of the train, hoping that that was the safest place to put her.

They decided that they should move now before the weather broke. They decided also to take a gamble and not head at an angle from their direction of travel to reach the nearest water hole line, but would rely on the rain coming and filling the dry holes that lay directly ahead of them. That was some gamble to take, for they were in a long dry spell and several times lately rain had threatened and not come. But both men knew the country well and both were pretty confident that rain would come in the next day or so. So they started to move directly south, both mildly surprised that Stratton had made no move against them. They had not travelled for more than a couple of hours over the plain when the weather broke. The wind blew from the north and brought with it a teeming rain that drenched the horseback riders to the skin within minutes. They hurriedly donned their fishes, but it was too late. They were wet to the skin. Hastily men fastened tarpaulins and wagon-covers as the rain drove into the vehicles. The weather turned cold and the mules plodded wretchedly on. The riders guarding the remuda of loose mules had their hands full keeping the animals together.

Mel rode up beside Arch and bellowed against the wind: "When I said rain would help us, I didn't mean this, by God."

When they halted at noon to rest the animals, the men chewed on cold tack and washed it down with water. Arch rode along the train to visit with Martha and eat a bite with her in the wagon perched on boxes of gold. She was remarkably cheerful and had dug a coat out of his warbag to keep him warm.

"I bet you wished you didn't come," he told her.

"Nothing of the kind," she said. "I wouldn't have missed it for worlds."

During the afternoon the rain continued to fall, but by nightfall it stopped and they were able to build Martha a fire so that she could cook an evening meal. They built the fires high and their soaked clothing steamed in the heat. The wagons were laagered and a strong guard set. They were on a waterhole and it was full. Their little gamble had paid off so far.

The next morning, they plodded on, their water containers full and every man feeling that they had made a good start. Every man that is excepting Ben Goodall who, still weak from the Apache arrow that he had taken, had not improved after the soaking he had received in the rain. He went down with a high fever and Arch wanted to lend him a horse to ride back into Crewsville where he could rest up. Ben refused hotly and Martha took him into her wagon to nurse him. Arch said no wonder he didn't want to ride back to Crewsville with that kind of treatment being metered out.

The day was dry, but threatening clouds still scudded overhead. They all agreed that this was no more than a lull in the rain. More would come, that was certain and when it came it would come hard. Still the going was soft from the rain of yesterday and there was water in the watercourses which had been dry for years. They were forced to cross several of these and it was not easy to find a hard bottom for the wagon wheels. Twice, they had wagons stuck fast and had to spend a valuable hour getting them free. But they headed south at a fairly steady pace, the mountains on their left hand coming steadily closer to them. They were so close now that men rode, turning their eyes to them frequently, wondering what danger there was there for them.

The nerves of the leaders were now becoming tight strung, for they all knew that the further south they went, the nearer they came to possible Apache ambush. And the danger not only could come from the left flank in the mountains, but from all around them. Mel and Arch knew, Charlie Garth knew that Apaches could lie hidden on the flat, could rise out of the bowels of the ground and surround a train in no time at all. Scouts were useless against them, they could ride out ahead, ride clean through the Indians without seeing them. But nevertheless, all three men, taking a rifleman with them for safety rode ahead and on the flanks in turn, probing possible cover and keeping a sharp eye for the concealing pits that the Apache liked to dig.

They nooned on a shrubless, waterless flat, resting the animals and giving the wagon-riders a chance to stretch their legs. All the time, there were men high on the wagons watching the country for any sign of movement. There was a brief break in the clouds and for a while the sun warmed them. But when they moved on in the afternoon, the rain came again, soaking the riders before they could slip their slickers on. They pushed on morosely, the wind driving behind them, which at least kept the stock moving willingly, for it was their instinct to go ahead of the wind.

Only after great difficulty did they manage to get a fire going for Martha that night, but she gave them some kind of a hot meal for which they were all grateful. She had changed her dress now for a pair of men's pants, which was the only wear possible in the rain and mud. But the woman seemed in high spirits and they all admired her for it. When a number of them were gathered around the fire to dry off that evening, Charlie Garth said: "Trouble's comin'. I can feel it in my water, beggin' your pardon, Mrs. Kelso, ma'am. Now when it comes, the rallying point, if'n we get scattered is Martha. Hear? Martha, if all hell breaks loose and we're all every which way, you scream a one hunnerd per centum woman's scream."

Martha protested strongly. She wasn't there to be a nuisance. The men had to look out for the gold.

They silenced her protests. They'd center on her scream.

Arch didn't say a thing.

They slept sitting up in a wagon that night, he and Martha, with one of his arms around her. They slept fitfully and once for a couple of hours, he went out to do his duty as a guard. Bedraggled and tired, she managed to cook them all a breakfast before dawn on the following morning, while the men sorted out the teams and hitched them to the wagons. They pushed on as soon as it was light with a driving rain behind them.

The mountains seemed ever closer now, pressing down gloomily on their left hand.

10

THEY drifted through the driving rain out
of town in ones and twos after midnight,
meeting in the inadequate shelter of the
cottonwoods on the bank of the creek, now full
of rushing water. It was so dark that the new
arrivals did not know they were at the
appointed spot until they had run into the
others. Men swore and horses shifted in the
darkness. Men sat wretchedly in their slickers
on wet saddles, water running down their
necks. All the Brand boys were there, Ringus
nervous at the idea of riding, even in so large
and well-armed a company, down into the
country of the Apache; another half-dozen men,
all carefully chosen by Doc Dooley for their
skill with firearms and their capacity for evil.
He had picked those who he knew to possess
some sense of loyalty to the man who hired
them. Not that he did not know that with the
amount of gold that was in that train that even
an honest man's loyalty might have been
strained to breaking point.

Doc came last of all, trotting over the muddy ground on his sure-footed, tall Kentucky mule. He halted and was at once all business, calling their names, checking that every man was there, making sure that the half-dozen pack mules were along. He dismounted and feeling with his hands in the dark made sure that they had been loaded to his liking.

Once more in the saddle, he asked: "Anybody backin' out? Do it now or forget about it. There won't be no backin' out from here on." Nobody wanted to back out.

But Dirk asked: "Where's the sense in tryin' it in all this rain, Doc? There won't be a track to see."

"You asked me that before," Doc said. "We're goin' now because the gold's out there now and available now. We wait for the sun, the gold could be gone. We're in this for gold. Witt, lead out."

Witt turned his horse and walked it down the bank into the waters of the creek. Saddle leather sounded softly through the rain as the men kneed their horses after him. Doc kept muttering: "Move out, move out. Get goin', for Crissake," as if he couldn't wait a moment longer to get on the trail after that gold. He counted the men as they passed him, patting the rain-wet rump of each horse as it went by. You couldn't be too sure, he told himself. He would need every man he had against Kelso and Dawford. He had seen some of their action and had heard more.

As the last man went down toward the creek, he got on the move himself, neck-reining his tall mule around and letting it find its own way down in the dark. The mule was the only creature Doc had met in life who never put a foot wrong.

The mule splashed through the water now, trumpeting a little because it wanted to be in front of the horses. Doc chuckled, some of the tension going out of him. Things were going to be all right. So long as nobody turned squeamish, this job was going to go all right. It had to be done thoroughly and without feeling. If one of those men ahead there in the darkness had any ideas about the sanctity of human life and the rest of that crap, the whole scheme could be ruined. Doc faced facts squarely. Every man in the gold-train had to be killed. Not one of them must live to tell the tale. There must be no evidence against Doc Dooley, not for a job this size.

But he had chosen his men carefully, knew every man jack of them. There wasn't one of them, by his reckoning who wouldn't have cut his own mother's throat for a poke of gold. Every man there was wanted in some State of the Union or other. However, Doc had not chosen them for their callousness alone. Each man could ride, shoot and had guts. Each man needed the money. Each man was physically hardy and would stand up to the rigors of the trip. And Doc wasn't fooling himself that that side of it, the mere riding and staying awake, was going to be easy.

His one worry was horses. The thought that he should have brought spares along nagged at him. But there had been no money for more horses. Every cent he could scrape together had been spent on arms and ammunition. He relied on the wagon-train to supply him with fresh stock.

He knew just what he was going to try and do. No, there was no try about it. He was going to succeed. He had to get the wagon-train as near to the Mexican border as he could. How long, he wondered, would it take him to get the gold to the border? If this weather kept up, the going would be heavy. If it got worse, the wagons could get bogged down. He sweated at the thought of hurrying those wagons with their heavy loads day after day to the border with maybe even the army after him. And he didn't have any doubts that, if news of his attack on the train reached the military he would have the cavalry and a bunch of Apache scouts breathing down his neck.

He jogged on through the rain, thinking, thinking, imagining himself and his men on a slow run away from the army. Aw, well, he thought, if the worse came to the worst, each man could pack a mule with gold and fog it for the border. A mule-pack of gold would keep a man in comfort for a long time and that was better than a slap in the belly with a wet fish. No, all he had to worry about was whether his men would wipe out Kelso and his crowd and silence them once and for all time. To do this, he had to pick his spot carefully. That in itself would not be easy, for he would bet a dime to a dollar that Kelso and Dawford wouldn't stick to the regular Crewsville - Tucson trail.

He thought about that. Maybe that wasn't a good bet after all. With this rain, the partners might stay on the trail because that would give them firmer going. Could be, could be.

Maybe he'd take a gamble and cut the trail about thirty miles south of here and scout it. He knew that would take him plump into the center of Apache country, but he knew he was risking an Indian fight any road.

He urged the mule forward with a touch of the spurs, trotted along the line of riders, all crouched down under the rain, and reached the head of the line. The big Kentucky mule snorted happily and stepped it out with a long, swinging, mile-eating pace.

A voice behind him said: "That you, Doc?"

That was Stet.

"Yeah," Doc said amiably. "How's it comin'?"

"It ain't comin' a-tall," Stet said. He hated water, inside or out. "Only thing that keeps me a-ridin' here is I'm plumb certain it's goin' to be me cuts Kelso down."

Doc chuckled.

"That's the kind of talk I like to hear," he said. "Keep thinkin' that all the time, boy."

They rode on through the night, every man there trusting Doc to find the way even though they could scarcely see the ears of their horses. Doc was a good man in wild places. Men said he had the nose, eyes and ears of an Apache.

He could home in the dark where skilled men could flounder. If the gold-train was up ahead there someplace, Doc would find it. He would fix it, just like he said, so they could knock off the train crew without getting themselves killed. They were all going to live to come out of this rich men.

11

IT had stopped raining.

Mules and men steamed in the weak sunlight. The whole desert seemed to throw up a damp and suffocating vapor as it started to dry out. But the going was still hard and the mules were straining at their loads. They changed the teams as frequently as they could when they stopped to rest, but they were holding to a hard pace and men began to wonder among themselves how long they could keep it up.

After crossing open desert, they had once again met the road and were travelling along it. The country here was not truly mountainous, but it was broken and the existence of cover for anybody who wanted to attack the train, gave the two partners some anxious thoughts. While the drivers watched their teams, the remainder of the men never took their eyes from the rocks, brush and ridges that reared and lunged on either hand.

Clouds raced overhead across a watery sky

and the breeze blowing from the north struck the men chill. But, though still wary and none of them unworried by the fact that they were now in country where they were liable to attack from both Indian and white cut-throats, the men were more cheerful. The mules were tired, but they were making good time. Sure, some of them were played out, but the train had come this far without any trouble. That night, they pulled off the road to the little settlement of Mescalero Springs. This had been started some years before as a road ranch and had developed into a fair-sized trading store. A blacksmith had settled there. Pretty soon it was a small community of some half-dozen houses and twenty people. Morgan Shade, who had run the ranch, was said to have done a good liquor trade with passing travelers and cattlemen. Upstairs, he had kept two Mexican girls, the only women for miles around at one time and they had earned him a comfortable income.

But this was all gone now, except for the burned out shells of the houses. Juanito had swooped down on the place from the hills the year before. By this time Shade and the girls had gone and with them had departed the majority of the inhabitants, either headed for the safety of Tucson or that of Crewsville. All that had been left had been a crazy boy who had declared that he wasn't afraid of any Indians alive and a crazier old man who had spent the last twenty years panning uselessly for gold in the hills. They had forted up in the store, but the Apaches had soon smoked them out of there. The story had it that the boy got away and died somewhere in the desert either of wounds or of thirst. The old man Juanito spreadeagled upside down on a wagon wheel and roasted his brains over a slow fire.

The place looked as desolate as only a deserted human habitation can. Dust had blown into the ruins of the houses, doors creaked eerily in the wind. Arch and Mel placed the wagons strategically among the houses and made a fortress of the place, using lumber from the houses to build good fires. They placed several riflemen out in the brush to listen and watch for intruders in the early part of the night, but when as the evening aged the sky cleared and the moon came out to improve visibility, they brought these men in and kept a strict watch from the perimeter of their camp. Arch and Martha made their rough bed in the ruins of a house and lay in fair comfort in each others arms, taking the opportunity not only to make love, but to talk of their prospects, what they would do if and when they safely reached Tucson. Arch still had terrible doubts in his mind about giving in to Martha and allowing her to come on the trip. There seemed to be no such doubt in her mind. She was the kind of woman who were making the West. She was gentle and feminine enough for any man, but she was a tough-minded woman for all that. She was with her man and he would look out for her. If he couldn't, she would look out for herself.

As they whispered together, a lobo howled dolefully in the hills and another answered from the plain. Some small creature of the night skuttled across the floor of the house. Outside came the slow steady tread of a guard.

"I didn't aim to give you this kind of honeymoon, girl," Arch said.

She snuggled her head into the comfort of his shoulder.

"We're together," she told him. "I don't ask for any more."

"What do we do when this is all over?" he said.

"What do you have in mind?"

"Land," he informed her. "I guess I never wanted to own anythin' but land. We could run cattle at first. But this ain't just cattle country. When it starts openin' up, there'll be more here than open cattle range. We lyin' on the top of water right here on this spot. There must be water under a hell of a lot of this country. All you have to do is have enough money to build the mills to bring it to the surface. An' I aim to do just that. Martha, in this climate and with water, you could raise anythin'. Garden truck, fruit, anythin'. I talked to a man in Tucson from the East. College man. A professor or somethin'. He reckoned that . . ."

They talked on, airing their dreams for the future. Arch fell asleep thinking about getting the train safely through to Tucson and making his stake.

12

THE sun was high and it was as hot as the pits of hell. Suddenly, soon after dawn, the sky had cleared and the wind had died down. In no time at all it was as if the rain had never been. From crouching miserably in their slickers under the tumult of the rain, the men were now reduced to seeking every small scrap of shade that was available.

Doc Dooley had halted them in what appeared to be a box canyon. That didn't look like good strategy to some of them, for once you were in a box canyon it wasn't easy to get out. Doc reasoned differently. He knew this country and he reckoned that he had chosen a spot where nobody would come. There was no reason to go there. There was no water, no brush or wood of any kind, nothing but rock and dust. But Doc had thought of everything. On the mules were not only spare ammunition; there was water and there was feed for the stock. So men and beast were able to slake their thirst and to fill their bellies. There was not enough for anybody to over-indulge, but there was enough.

Doc himself had taken a half-breed Mohave Indian named Joe Price with him and ridden south-west, telling the men that he would be back before nightfall. They and the animals were to get all the rest they could. Tomorrow there would be hard riding. They believed him and they rested. They were glad to after the night ride that extended itself right through the dawn and on into the early morning.

True to his word, Doc rode into the canyon shortly before dark. He trotted in on a Kentucky mule that was as fresh as when it had set out. Joe Price's mustang was bushed. Doc was pleased with himself and he showed it. He dismounted with a kind of fat flourish, threw the lines to Joe and sat himself down on a rock. He was covered in dust from head to foot, he was unshaven and his eyes were bloodshot from sun-glare and dust, but he looked what he was: a man who controlled men, a man who could make other men afraid of him even though they might be better with a gun, quicker with a knife or handier with their fists and feet. Being what he was, he didn't seek the men out to tell them his news—he waited for them to come to him.

And they came. In fact, as soon as he came in sight, every man there was on his feet. They wanted to know if they would get the gold; they wanted to know how quickly they would be leaving this oven of a canyon.

Doc lit a cigar and beamed on them all as if he were a loving father and they were his children.

Witt Brand made an impatient sound.

"Well," he said, "what did you find?"

"The train, of course, boy. Isn't that what I rid out for? Joe . . . Joe, where the hell're you at? Joe, tell 'em just how long it took for me to locate that train."

Joe grunted and grimaced. That was his way of grinning.

"You sure fin' him damn quick, Doc. Goddam, but quick."

Ringus said: "You see 'em plain? How close did you git?"

Doc looked at him in some astonishment.

"See it? What in hell did I want for to see it, man?" he snorted.

"You mean you never seed it?"

"Jesus, Ringus, ain't there no limit to your foolishness? Did I want Kelso and Dawford to see my dust? Joe an' me drifted along nice an' easy around a couple or three hours behind the train. We took a look around the Wells. Read sign. Plain as the palm of your hand. They was there last night. I know what speed they're travellin' at. I know the road they're takin'. I know right when to hit 'em."

Rod Brand said eagerly: "Tonight. We could jump them camped."

Doc made a noise of disgust.

"We ain't doin' no sech thing," he said. "We do it in daylight. We gotta see 'em, don't we? Ain't I told you and told you, not one of them bastards has to get away. They all gotta be plumb dead. Just one gets away and that could be the end of us. You all got that."

They murmured that they got it. Men glanced at each other, wondering if they all had the iron in them to do it.

Doc looked at them from under the shadow of his hat.

"Anybody doubt you can do it? I don't want nobody with doubts. You can't do it, I'll be big-hearted about it. Jest climb on your horse an' ride."

They all denied any human weakness.

"Good," Doc said and he looked proud of

158

them as if each one of them were his own creation.

Joe Price spat. He was a tall angular man of indeterminate age with a face like a brown gargoyle. The way he used a knife was pure artistry.

"One of 'em," he said, "was a woman."

There was silence. Everybody there looked first at Joe and then shifted their gaze to Doc Dooley.

For a moment, Doc looked murderous. No one there would have been surprised to have seen him draw his belt-gun and kill Joe Price. As quickly as the look had come, it went. Doc never lost control of himself for long without purpose.

Quietly, he said: "You must be crazy, Joe. There ain't no woman with the train."

Just as quietly and with a strange confidence that reached out to the listeners, Joe said: "You know I ain't crazy, Doc. I read sign. I know a woman was at the Wells."

Doc stood up and faced the half-breed.

"You read sign pretty good, Joe," he said. "I'll give you that. We all know it. But you think you read sign better 'n me? You think that?"

"I know what I see."

Doc appealed to the men.

"What man would be crazy enough to take a woman on a trip like this?"

A man dressed in worn range clothes and with the grime of years on him, but with a spotlessly clean gun on his hip, spoke.

"Kelso would. If'n that new wife of his'n talked him into it. That's who I reckon it is."

Doc raised his voice a little.

"We watched the train leave, didn't we? Did anybody see a woman on it?"

A man who looked like an itinerant cowhand said: "She could of been in one of the wagons. We all know she rid out to the camp. Miz Martha's the kind to go along. If'n Joe's right an' there's a woman there, it'll be Miz Martha."

That murderous look flashed across Doc's face momentarily again.

"All right," he said. "We can't stand here arguin' all day. So—there's a woman on the train. Does that make any difference?"

A tall man with a broken nose and a scar down one side of his face, spoke out of the deep shade of his Mexican sombrero—

"Not to me, it don't."

Doc looked around at the faces of the other

men. This was the one thing he hadn't reckoned on. He had aimed at killing men. Killing women wasn't the same thing. Not to men in this country. Too many of them had grown up with the idea that a woman was a valued thing, possessing the exalted value of a scarce commodity. They had discarded every other moral law, but some of them had retained their respect for women. Doc knew it at once. He hesitated, debating whether to get tough or to reason with them.

He decided to try reason first.

He sat down again and relit the cigar that had gone out. The men stood motionless, waiting for him to speak, some of them for the first time feeling a distaste for the bloody task that lay ahead of them.

Doc spoke.

"All right," he said. "I ain't sayin' I agree with Joe there's a woman on the train. But if he's right an' I'm wrong, an' I ain't never been wrong yet over sign, then what do we do because there's a woman along. Call the whole thing off? Just turn around an' go back?" He drew on the cigar and blew smoke into the air. "So—there's wagon-loads of gold down there on the Tucson trail. Even if we take as much

161

as every man here can carry, we each have more gold than any of you fellers'll get within sniffin' distance of for the rest of your lives. Think about that. Think good, but don't spend too much time on it. You don't never have to work again. You don't never have to be short of nothin'. Never."

They stayed still, watching him.

The cowhand said: "I can use the gold. We all can. We ain't arguin' about that. It just sticks in a man's craw to kill a woman. There ain't no arguin' about that either."

Dirk Brand, who had a wife he was crazy about, said: "I'll kill anythin' that moves. Anythin'. Barrin' a woman."

Doc looked again from face to face. He would have liked to know what was going on in their minds. He got to his feet and walked away from them, hands behind his back and coat-tails flapping. To anybody who didn't know him, he would have looked a comic figure. He didn't look comic to any of the men there. They all feared him.

He went twenty paces and came back again, glaring at them and tossing the half-smoked cigar aside.

"So we got some soft ones among us," he

said. "You make me puke. You make me Goddam sick to my stomach."

Joe Price said: "You want the woman killed, Doc, you do it."

Doc swung on him.

"Christ," he shouted, "is that all that's frettin' you. You think I can't do it? All right —I kill the woman. Does that help any? Could you stand seein' a poor defenseless woman killed?" He banged himself on the chest. "I'll do it. Does that make it better for you lily-livered sonsabitches?"

They shuffled their feet, some looked at the ground, ashamed of their squeamishness.

"So, it's settled," he said. "Saddle your horses and let's get outa here."

They paused a moment, as if still thinking about the woman who was going to be killed, hitched their belts and moved slowly to the horse line. There was not a word spoken. Every man there, even those who had no objection to killing a woman, were slightly awed by the thought of what Doc would do.

Doc turned to Joe Price.

"You would have to open your Goddamed mouth," he said.

Softly, Joe said: "You knowed there was a woman there."

Doc snarled: "You think I'm blind?"

He turned and tramped to the Kentucky mule and heaved himself gracelessly into the saddle, bellowing for the men to get a move on, they didn't have all day.

In five minutes, they were lined out, walking their horses down the canyon. Not long after, they entered a small valley that seemed to be composed of nothing but dry brush, cactus and dust. The air was slightly cooler now, but still hot. The men sighed with relief to get out of the furnace of the canyon. Doc lifted the mule into its long swinging trot.

The valley took them south for several hours and led them to a barren and stoney plain. Doc turned the mule and swung west across this. It was dark now and nobody knew where they were. They all felt helpless and entirely in Doc's hands. But they trusted him to get them faultlessly to the train. Around midnight, he called a halt and they rested the animals for an hour. They didn't unsaddle, but did no more than loosen girths. Some men took sips of water from their canteens, but Doc went around telling them to go easy on water, he didn't know when they'd be getting more.

The hour up, Doc struck a lucifer and looked at his watch. He grunted and told them to mount up. The pace he hit now was brisker and men started to say that they were worried about the horses giving out. When one man mentioned his thoughts to Doc, he was told that there was fresh stock up ahead. They had to get into position for the attack before daylight. The surprise had to be complete. Kelso and Dawford were pretty smart boys and the fellows with them could all fire a gun, that was why they had been hired.

Three hours before dawn, Doc swung first south and then south-east. An hour later he stopped and told them that they were on the Tucson trail. He took them across the trail and halted them about a quarter mile to the east of it. Giving the order to off-saddle, to eat and get what rest they could, he set his sentries and walked off into the night.

Shortly before dawn, he was back, in among them without the sentries spotting him. It seemed to give him innocent delight to sneer at them for not stopping him.

"If'n I was an Injun," he told them, "I'd

of cut a few throats before you knowed I was here."

He told them to saddle up and follow him. Mounting his mule, he led them back toward the trail and once again halted. Now he had a couple of the packs broken out and issued each man with an extra supply of ammunition. He then detailed two men to stay with the animals.

"When I shout for them horses," he said, "you come arunnin'. Fast. We ain't goin' to let them fellers fort up. Any sign of there bein' a stand off and we ride in. This has to be quick. Now, I'm dividin' the rest of you into two parties. One on either side of the trail." He named men off. "You go for the leaders. I want one leader in each team downed right at the start so they can't corral. Them wagons has to stop dead."

Rod Brand said: "Don't we need them teams?"

"They got spares along. You think I'm stupid or somethin'? All right, let's go."

They pushed on into the darkness until Doc halted them again, naming the men he wanted to stay on this side of the trail. He walked along the ridge they were on and positioned each man individually. He had not seen this spot, but had walked it carefully in the dark, seeing only in his mind's eye the lines of fire and the amount of cover each man would have. When he had placed all the men, he paced stolidly back to the other group and led them across the road. These men he took onto higher ground and also placed one by one, telling them that there might be a wait of several hours, but if one of them took it into his head to show himself, he'd have that head off his shoulders when this was over. Not one of them who heard the threat took it lightly. They all knew Doc.

That done, Doc walked north along the trail for about two hundred yards and took up a position on raised ground that he guessed would give him a long view of the road when daylight came. He lay flat to light a cigar. Maybe it wasn't wise, because an Indian could have picked up the scent over a mile down wind. But he needed a smoke and, hell, who was worried about Indians at that moment?

Dawn came.

Doc found that he had chosen his spot well and it wasn't long before he had a pretty good view of several miles of the road. He inspected the ridges where he had positioned his men and found to his satisfaction that he could not see hide or hair of one of them.

He lit another cigar. He was hungry, but he knew that he was too tensed up to eat. The fact that he was tense didn't worry him. He was used to it. Always at times like this, when other men looked at him and wondered at his being so calm, his nerves were screaming in protest. But he had learned to live with the torture of it. The first shot that went off would be the signal for his nerves to settle down. His mind would clear itself then and work like clockwork. He knew that when the time came he would keep his nerve and see this thing through to the end. In a short while now, he would be leading a gold train south toward the border.

He finished the cigar and ground the butt out on a stone. He thought about the gold and he started to feel a little gay. He smiled gently to himself.

Suddenly, he stiffened.

Was that a whiff of dust his sharp eyes had caught to the north?

He raised himself a little. Could be. He took a small glass from his pocket and extended it. He did not find the dust at once, but suddenly there inside the circle was a moving speck.

There was dust there, all right, and something was on the road making it. All he had to do was make sure what it was. He hoped to God his hopes weren't being raised by some daring lone traveller or a party of Indians. He put down the glass and rested his eye.

A terrible thought hit him. Maybe he had been over-sure of himself and had made a mistake. Maybe the train had been moving faster than he had calculated and had passed this spot. He hadn't been able to check that in the dark. Maybe he'd been too smart by half.

But when he put the glass to his eye again a few minutes later, he knew that he had not been wrong.

Plainly now, he could see the moving line of animals and the wagon behind. Dimly, behind that, almost lost in the dust was another wagon.

He scrambled to his feet and walked down the hill. He wanted to run and shout his triumph to the men, but that would never do. He must appear calm and confident to them. He rounded the western ridge and told the men: "Here they come. Won't be long now."

He gave a whistle on his fingers. A head popped up on the other side of the trail and he made a sign to the man with his hand. The man signalled back that he understood.

Men started looking to their rifles, checking the loads for the heaven knew how many times. He looked at their faces and knew that he hadn't been mistaken in them. They were all fighting men and they would fight. Nothing like greed to give men backbone. Pity Joe had to open his mouth about that damned woman.

They waited.

Suddenly, the pre-attack nerves started among the men. They began to swallow frequently, hands moved nervously. But he knew that, like him, they'd be all right as soon as the shooting started.

He could see the train now with the naked eye, a dark thread winding slowly along the gully of the road, mules plodding steadily, one or two riders out on either hand.

Doc prayed the riders stayed right there with the wagons and did not come scouting ahead. One rider only had to take it into his head to ride off to one side of the road for a look around and the gold could be lost to him. Doc knew that he didn't have enough men with him to beat Kelso and Dawford without the element of surprise.

The train crept closer.

A mile.

A half-mile.

The sun was hot overhead now.

A quarter-mile.

Suddenly, Doc swore.

What he had feared, had happened. One of the horseback riders had left the train and was coming ahead at a brisk canter. In a few minutes, the hidden men heard the thud of the horse's hoofs on the hard trail. Men turned their heads to look questioningly at Doc.

It was Kelso.

Doc stared at the lone horseman with bitter hatred. Then he switched his eyes to the train. It was within rifle shot now. Maybe luck was with Doc. Maybe even if Kelso spotted them they could throw down on the train and get away with it.

Doc ducked down. Kelso was swinging his gaze this way and that. Doc heard the horse's hoofbeats almost opposite him. There came a scrabble of loose stones. Hastily, Doc raised his head and saw to his horror that Kelso had turned his horse to the other side of the trail and was urging it up the ridge behind which his other party of men were hidden.

Doc's mind hovered for a brief moment between gunning Kelso down and opening fire on the leaders of the first team.

Kelso would die whether Doc fired at the train or him first. Therefore—the train.

Doc levered a round into the breech of his repeater and slammed the brass-bound butt into his shoulder. Quickly, he sighted on the off lead mule. The shot was not a difficult one.

13

ARCH would never know what instinct, if indeed it were instinct at all, that made him call out to Mel: "I'm ridin' ahead. I don't like them ridges close to the trail like that."

Mel nodded. Arch turned in the saddle to lift a hand to Martha sitting beside the driver of her wagon. She returned the salute and flashed him a smile. He lifted the bay to a trot and then a canter, going past the lead wagon. Suddenly, for no accountable reason, he felt a tension in the air. He looked around him. Nothing stirred. The sun beat down mercilessly on an arid landscape; the dust of the trail, yesterday's rain quickly dried out, threw the glare up into his face and he squinted his eyes against it.

There were high ridges on either side of the trail. Something in him told him that if there were danger anywhere, it must be on the other side of one of those ridges. This, of all the places they had passed on the road, was the ideal place for an ambush. From here on to

Tucson, there would be no better spot than this for the purpose of a hold-up.

He neck-reined the bay to the left and it slowed its pace as it hit the bottom of the steep gradient. Bunching its hindlegs it thrust itself up and forward. It balked at an extra steep place, Arch touched it with the spurs and spoke to it.

Just then, the shot came.

It came from behind him.

His heart gave an almighty thump and he reined the animal around. His sudden jump of nerves must have made him handle the beast's soft mouth roughly. The animal backed and pitched once.

Arch caught sight of the wisp of dark smoke on the other side of the trail high up on the ridge.

There came the stutter and crash of several rifles and the ridge top was marked with small puffs of dark smoke.

Arch heard himself exclaim: "Christ!"

The ridge behind him seemed to erupt with the sound of rifle fire and the air around-him was alive with flying lead. He jerked his head toward the train and saw that the lead team was in a shambles.

For a moment, his mind was blank with panic. Martha and the train there, him here, a wall of lethal lead in between. Any second a bullet would smack into him and he would be in the dust, dead.

Something tore his hat from his head. He ducked voluntarily too late. Every nerve in his body screamed for escape. Something struck the saddlehorn and the bay staggered under him. He thought the animal was hit and knew that his only chance was to make the horse run before it went down. It might get him a short way clear.

He jammed the spurs home and yelled to the bay. It jumped. Sideways on to the slope now, it slipped and Arch thought it was going down. The rifles were hammering away above him. By sheer good horsemanship and pure desperation, he kept the horse on its feet, then he tore home the spurs again and the animal angled down the slope, half-running and half-sliding. There was a pain in the back of his arm like a red-hot needle. The bay hit the trail going south and away from the train, Arch lying along its neck, spurring and yelling. Dust spurted ahead of him as lead hit the trail. It seemed that he raced along for an eternity with the crash of rifle fire in his ears.

Then, abruptly, the sound of the firing was distant. The bay was still running freely and he was clear. A terrible constriction across his chest was released. He let the air sing out of his straining lungs. He was still alive.

It didn't seem possible.

His mind switched to Martha back there in that storm of gunfire. Turning in the saddle, he saw that men were on the ridge-top running. A rush of movement in the east caught his eye—riders were coming with led horses, hurrying them untidily over the rough ground. The train was now hidden from his sight. The bay came down to a trot and he turned it right. In seconds he had a ridge between himself and the attacking force. He used the spurs again, urgent to get back to Martha. Nothing mattered now but Martha. They could have all the gold in the world and he wouldn't stop them. He had to save Martha. Too late to regret bitterly that he had allowed her to come on this trip.

The bay was limping.

Mercilessly, Arch spurred it again and it did its best to respond. The pace slowed as they climbed a ridge and part of the battle came in sight; the sounds of it too: the stutter of rifle-fire, the shouting of men and the scream of a horse or mule as it went down in its death agony.

The bay slid down the ridge side and the battle disappeared again. Arch wiped the sweat from his face and rode, going as fast as he dared over the tricky ground, praying the bay would not go down before they reached the train.

They hit a flat and the western ridge the attackers were on came in sight again. He could see the men up there clearly. For a moment nobody spotted him in the noise and heat of the fight, but before he came around the west side of the ridge and spotted the train a man saw him and opened up on him. The range was long, but the bullets came close. Too close for comfort. But he was desperate to reach the train and held to his course. Another man caught sight of him and started pumping shots his way.

As he approached it, he saw that the train was in a state of utter confusion. The men had tried to laager in too confined a space and the result was chaotic. Teams seemed to be entangled, one wagon had mounted a ridge at the side of the road and gone over, the team fighting insanely to free itself. There was a horseman riding up and down, waving an arm and shouting. Arch thought that was Mel. Men fought to hold the heads of the leaders, others were under the wagons firing. As he came nearer a man ran out from the wagons, flung himself flat on the ground at the side of the trail and started shooting up at the ridges.

The bay thundered on. Arch bracing himself as if he were charging into an inferno. The bay broke stride, Arch was jerked violently in the saddle and the next moment the animal went from under him and he was sailing through the air. Instinctively, he had managed to kick his feet free of the stirrup-irons, but he was too confused to land on his feet. He tried to come down running, but failed, tripping on his own feet and crashing to the ground, dropping his rifle as he did so.

For a moment, he lay half-stunned, but the urgency of the situation drove him to his feet, groping for the rifle.

The bay lay a few yards away on one side, kicking and screaming.

Arch worked the lever of the rifle, aimed and fired. The bay lay still.

The horse was no sooner dead than Arch was on his feet, running, stumbling on the uneven ground. The men on the ridges were firing at him still. To his horror, he saw a man among the wagons shooting in his direction. He waved a hand as he ran shouting at the top of his voice, trying vainly to be heard over the sound of the firing.

The man on the horse stopped his frantic riding and yelling. The horse stumbled and went down onto its knees and the rider lurched from the saddle. Both seemed to thresh about on the ground. The horse finally reared to its feet and ran off past Arch. The man got to his feet and stumbled in a blind circle, hands to his face. As Arch drew near he saw that the hands and the head were covered in blood. He also saw that it was Mel.

A women was screaming. That would be Martha. He caught Mel by an arm as he came up to him, turned him and pushed him in the direction of the nearest wagon. The din was deafening. He was thrusting Mel under a wagon. He saw a woman's face near the wheel and realised it was Martha. Her face was covered with dust and her hair was all over the place. He shouted to her to keep down. He ran around the wagon onto the trail and collided with Charlie Garth.

Garth bawled: "They're mounting up. They're goin' to rush us."

Ben Goodall was climbing over the tailboard of a wagon.

A man stumbled in the middle of the trail, went to his knees and slowly slid down on his face. One foot kicked gently.

Arch saw that the overturned wagon was on the further side of the trail. Another was close to it and the two teams were all in a tangle, living and dead mules. The spare mules had run for it back down the trail away from the terrifying sound of the guns. The remainder of the wagons were bunched untidily together and here were the bulk of the men.

Garth ran on, bellowing that the bushwhackers were coming in.

Arch looked up the trail and saw the riders coming down from the ridge around to the west of the wagons. They streamed down one after the other and for the first time he saw that they were whitemen. The firing had stopped suddenly and a stunning silence lay over the scene. Gunsmoke drifted lazily on the hot air.

Arch got a grip on himself and walked around to the other side of the wagons so that he could have a clear view of the advancing riders. They were taking their time. He looked at his own men and could see no more than a half dozen. Had so many been downed in the first burst of firing? It didn't seem possible.

"All right, boys," he said. "I reckon they're goin' to rush us. Hold your fire till I say."

Martha was staring at him as if she couldn't believe that he was alive. She had a rifle in her hands.

"Get under cover, Arch," she called, "and don't be a fool."

"I'm all right, honey," he said. He found that he was quite calm now. He wanted to be in the open so that he would have an unrestricted view of the attackers and his movements would not be confined by a wagon. Those men would be riding hard and wouldn't be able to hit a damn thing. A cool man on foot could knock two or maybe three out of the saddle before they were among the wagons.

One of the riders was shouting orders and waving an arm about. There was something familiar about the man, but the distance was too great to recognise the man.

Suddenly, the line of horsemen split, one half streaking at a flat run back toward the trail, the other half appearing to intend to ride past the wagons.

"Charlie," Arch called to Garth, "you cover the trail."

Garth answered cheerily.

A man came and stood out in the open with Arch, three or four yards to his right. It was Ben Goodall.

"Start shootin', man," he said.

Arch said: "No, hit 'em with a volley when they turn into us. That'll stop 'em."

"You'll have to kill 'em to stop 'em. There never was so much gold in one place for the havin'."

He raised his rifle to his shoulder, took careful aim and fired. The leading horse went down in a flurry of kicking legs. The sound of the pitiful neigh came to them. The other riders swept past the fallen rider as he staggered to his feet. Ben levered quickly and fired again. The man spun around and went down.

A single shout came from the riders and they all turned in toward the wagons. Arch could hear the other party thundering down the trail.

Charlie Garth shouted an order and rifles crackled.

Arch let the riders facing him get to within a

hundred yards and called: "Now." He raised his rifle and started shooting. Lead poured out from the wagons. But the riders came on seemingly unscathed. They were all riding with the lines in their teeth and rifles firing as they charged nearer. Something quailed within Arch and suddenly he felt hoplessly vulnerable in the open. Suddenly there were riders within twenty yards of him and already he could feel the terrible impact of the horses hitting him, the iron hoofs pounding his flesh. For one anguished moment, his mind flicked to Martha behind him and he knew then why he was out in the open here. For no other reason than to stop these men reaching her.

There was a horse and rider right on top of him.

He fired and threw himself to one side.

The horse rushed by, smashed into the side of a wagon and the man fell from the saddle as helpless as a rag doll.

Then there was the turmoil and dust of horses being hastily turned and they all thundered on away from the wagons.

Arch stood dazed for a moment.

Turning, he looked to where Martha had been. She was still there under the wagon on her knees, a smoking rifle in her hands, her face black with powder. The man by her lay on his face. The side of the wagon and its canvas had been ripped and torn by lead.

"They paid for that," Ben said.

Arch heard the other party of riders go down the trail. He walked along the wagons, stopped and watched the two parties meet and stop. There were two men under the end wagons.

"Watch 'em," he said. "Sing out if they move."

He walked back to the wagon under which Martha crouched. There an attacker and his horse lay motionless. Two more men and a horse lay a short distance away. Their leader had lost his head. He should have kept his men in good cover and slowly whittled the wagon-train crew down. He could have had them all dead by sundown. But he was in a hurry. He wanted this over and done with. He wanted to be hurrying south with the gold. It didn't matter how many men he lost. Not so long as he had enough men to move the gold south.

Arch walked up to Mel where he lay on the ground. He lay on his back and his eyes were open. What the bullet had done to his face was indescribable and unforgettable. It was covered with blood and the dust had settled on it.

"Mel," Arch said and dropped to one knee beside his friend. He thought the eyes turned in an effort to see him, but he couldn't be sure. He imagined that the lips moved very slightly. But he was mistaken. When he felt for a pulse beat, there was none. Mel was dead.

Arch stood up. It was a desecration to leave Mel lying there in the dust, but there wasn't time to move him. Mel and the other men lying there, the members of the train crew who died in the dust, had died because of the gold. He stood still for a moment, hating the treasure he carried in the wagons with a terrible bitterness that wracked him like a physical pain. In that minute, he felt like abandoning the gold, getting what men he could onto the backs of mules and riding out of there, trusting to the gold to hold the raiders on the spot, to prevent them from pursuit. But he had been given a trust and he had never in his life failed a brand that hired him. The code was a simple one for a crude frontier and it was one he believed in.

It was strange standing there with Mel dead, without Mel to help him come to a decision. Mel hadn't ruled him or anything like that, but somehow he had gotten used to sharing decisions with his partner. So he had to make his own mind up now, alone. Maybe he was called upon to share such things with Martha now, but he knew he would not share this decision with her, because she would let her feelings for him rule her decision. And he knew what he had to do and he meant to do it.

He decided.

He walked back to the wagons and raised his voice so that all the men could hear him.

"Boys," he said, "we hold 'em off till dark. We can do it. There ain't so many of 'em now. We have all the ammunition in the world."

Garth asked: "What do you aim to do after dark, Arch?"

"Get on the mules and head out."

From under the wagon came a man's shocked voice—

"An' leave the gold?"

Arch said: "You think a few bars of gold're worth more'n your life."

Ben Goodall came up, looking pale and sick.

"We was hired to get this gold to Tucson, Arch." There was mild rebuke in his voice. Arch knew the feeling behind it wasn't mild.

Ben was a dangerous man and a wild one, but he was so honest it hurt.

Arch looked at him.

In a low voice so that Martha couldn't hear him: "We'll get the gold to Tucson, Ben. Trust me."

Ben gave him a side-eyed look.

Arch raised his voice: "Will, an' you, George, watch them jaspers. Shoot as soon as they get within range. The rest of you give me a hand with these teams."

They got to work, cutting out the dead leaders and moving the wagons in a rough circle. It was hard hot work in the burning sun. To the north, the riders sat their horses watching them, apparently not moving. Maybe they were arguing over whether to try another rush again. If they had any sense, they wouldn't.

They didn't. Slowly they walked their horses across the trail and over the ridge to the east, disappearing. Arch knew that they would work their way along the ridge and before long would be dropping lead down into the laager. He ordered: "Charlie, take Will and George and get up on that ridge. Warm 'em up a mite till we get through here. An' don't get yourselves hit."

Charlie and the two men ran across the trail and started up the ridge. Arch and the others who were not wounded started unloading some of the crates of gold from the wagons, building a low wall with them. It would offer the defenders protection till dark and slow the departure of the raiders after Arch and his crew had pulled out. Every little delay would help.

Charlie and his men started firing from the top of the ridge.

14

IT was dark; the blackness of the night seemed alight with the rage of Doc Dooley. He lay on the ridge seeing the pale blur that was the canvas of the wagons immediately below him. He lay there and thought impotently of the great fortune that lay there ready for his hand. He felt that it was so close that all he had to do was to stretch out that hand to touch it. Yet those stubborn fools down there still stood in his way. It seemed impossible. He knew that he had killed a great many of them, but the job had not been half-done. All that he had intended, all that he had carefully planned had not happened. He himself had suffered three dead and two wounded. There were left barely enough men to keep the defenders pinned down. Why, the three men whom Kelso had put on the ridge-top had held out for more than an hour before they had been driven below to the shelter of the wagons.

He knew that his own men were shaken. It was only his strength of character that had stopped them from running out on him. They were tough enough, and to them human life was the cheapest commodity on the market, yet three dead had shaken them. They had come on this trip for quick and easy profit, not for death. Two of them were wounded, but they were here on the ridge, reluctant to give up their chance at the gold.

Doc was worried as well as enraged.

Several possibilities were on his mind.

One, Kelso might send somebody riding out into the night for help. Two, he might stay with the wagons and continue the fight and a passing army patrol might come up to investigate. Three, Arch might pull out himself and head successfully for Tucson. That could bring authority out on Doc's trail.

So, he either had to kill all the people down there with the train or he had to get away with what gold he could carry at speed.

He found that he was sweating profusely.

He had to stop anybody getting away from the train. Anybody. But he also had to hold this high ground above the train. That was the only advantage he did hold.

"Dirk," he called.

The others passed the man's name down the

line and the big fair man came walking along to Doc, dropping on one knee beside him. Doc couldn't see his face in the gloom and he wished he could. He would have liked to see all the faces of the men, to know what their feelings were, what risks they would take.

"What is it?" Dirk asked. Doc thought there was an irritable edge to his voice.

"You take Joe Price and cover the way west. Kelso could break out that way."

"What if he makes a break down the road?"

"Too risky. We have that covered."

"But you don't really think he's goin' to leave all that gold."

"I don't believe he has any choice. Least he won't have when the moon comes up."

Dirk was silent, as though he were considering the worth of Doc's idea. This was something that had never happened before.

"All right," he said, finally. "But, Doc, we have to have that gold fast. We ought to be outa here and long gone by the dawn. We don't have all the time in the world, you know."

Doc snapped: "Don't you tell me, boy. I know what we have to do an' what we don't. You git down there and do your part an' I'll do mine."

Dirk sucked his breath in.

"Keep your hair on," he said and stood up. He walked along the ridge, calling Joe Price by name. A moment or two later, Doc heard them moving back in the darkness and reaching their horses. They rode out in an easy walk and Doc knew that the small sound would not reach the men with the wagon train with the ridge in the way. The two riders went north and quickly their sounds died away. Doc waited impatiently for the moon. As soon as the moon was up, he would pour lead down into the wagons so that a man down there dare not lift his head. He had all the ammunition in the world and to spare. With this fire being maintained he would have men down on the trail to outflank the defenders from the south. He hadn't too many men to play with, but he had enough. He wanted all those people down there dead and he was going to see them dead. Most of all he wanted Kelso. He knew that Dawford had been either killed or seriously wounded. That left only Kelso to lead. Without him, the defence would die the death.

But he never made his move. Kelso moved first.

Arch Kelso knew that he had made up his

mind. Nothing would turn him from his purpose now. He knew exactly what was going to happen as if he had the power to ordain the future. He knew that he was risking his life, but he had the confidence that he would come through. He would get Martha out of this alive, he would retain the gold and he would come back alive to Martha. He had to. It was something he had come to believe in the bitter hours since Mel had died.

All he needed was some luck. A hell of a lot of luck.

The men by and under the wagons were still, listening for movement from the men they knew to be still on the ridge. They were all tired. Under constant, though distant fire, they had laboriously dug shallow graves in the hard ground for their dead. Eight men had been rolled into blankets and put into that ground. Eight men lay under dirt and dust over which mules had been walked to hide the graves as best the men knew how. That left Arch with six men fit to fight and four badly wounded. It was the wounded men who worried him. He did not have to be told that the attackers would not hesitate to kill them if they were left. If he managed to slip away, taking whole and wounded men with him, he would not be able to leave the wounded in the desert. There would be acute danger for them not only from the men on the ridge, but from Indians. For never did the Indian threat leave Arch's mind. His party would be weak and encumbered by wounded. He had to take his wounded all the way to Tucson and safety. Two of them should have a doctor to care for them or they would die.

Young Joe Debson called: "Arch, there's horses movin' to the west."

They all listened.

Arch heard first the soft sound of bridle chains and then the soft thud of horses' hoofs as they walked.

"Ben," he said, "you crawl out a ways and keep your eyes skinned."

Ben said: "Keno," and crawled away into the darkness.

Charlie Garth called: "Sounds like a couple of fellers crossing the trail to the south."

Arch said: "Keep watchin', Charlie."

He started to worry. The attackers were moving before him. If he waited much longer, he could be too late.

He said: "I ain't goin' to raise my voice. Can

194

you all hear me?" They murmured assent. "Can you hear me, Charlie?"

"Yeah. Go ahead."

He cleared his throat, paused for a moment as he wondered not for the first time how the men would take the idea of pulling out, how Martha would take it.

"We're pullin' out," he told them.

He felt their reaction to the news.

"My God," Charlie Garth said. "You know what you're doin', man?"

"I know what I'm doin'."

"We hired out to guard this gold," Charlie said. "We been paid to see it gets to Tucson. We don't get it there not one of us has a stake."

Arch said: "There's eight men in the ground who won't never have a stake again. I don't aim to have any more that way."

Martha said: "You know what you're doin', Arch?" He knew that he had shocked her.

"I know what I'm doin'," he said for the second time. "There's more ways of killin' a coyote than shootin' it."

"What's on your mind?"

"Plenty. And it's stayin' right there."

He could imagine Charlie's reaction to the

rebuff. He had told the older man to mind his own business.

Charlie said: "When I'm hired, I'm hired. We can stand these jaspers off. Hell, we killed some of 'em. They ain't feelin' too good right now, I'll bet. They ain't tried to rush us again. We hurt 'em. We been hired to stay with this gold an' I vote we stay with it."

"You have my word," Arch said. "This gold'll get to Tucson."

Young Joe Debson said: "I ain't tryin' to fight you, Arch. You're the boss. But how in heck do you aim to get this gold to Tucson if we make a break for it?"

"Leave that to me."

"Arch," Martha said, "you aiming to do something crazy? I know you." Her voice shook a little. She was afraid for him.

"We're goin' to come out of this all right," Arch told her. "You'll have to trust me."

Garth said: "Nobody ain't sayin' they don't trust you, Arch. Hell, we all know you. But I can't see how you can get the gold to Tucson if we ride out and leave it."

Arch's patience reached its limit. The tension rose in him.

"For Gawd's sake," he said. "We don't have

much time. Like Joe said: I'm the boss here. We'll do like I say. I guarantee every man his pay. I'll guarantee we get the gold to Tucson. That's all I'm sayin'."

Reluctantly, Charlie said: "This ain't the time for every man pulling every which way. Go ahead. I ain't feelin' so Goddam happy about anythin', but go ahead."

"All right," Arch said. "George, watch the south. Will, the ridge. You see any movement, you fire. Charlie an' the rest of you, I want a mule for every man. Saddle every animal you have a saddle for."

Charlie came out from under a wagon.

"What about the wounded men?"

"We ain't leavin 'em. These fellers would kill 'em."

Martha joined them.

"Arch, these men couldn't stay on a mule."

"Tie 'em on."

They tried to protest, but he over-rode them. He had made up his mind and nothing was going to stop him. He would get all these men and Martha safely to town and he would save the gold. There was nothing more to be said.

"The rest of the mules," he said. "Scatter 'em."

That would hold the attackers up for a while. They couldn't move the wagons without mules and they couldn't move the gold without wagons.

"Now," he added, "when you done that, break open a crate of gold and tie a bar on every mule we take with us. At least we'll have something to show for our trip when we reach town."

They started work, cutting the mules out of the traces. Their movement must have been heard from above, for the men up there started dropping lead into the train. But they couldn't see what they were shooting at and in the hour it took to get ready only one man received a slight flesh wound. When they were ready, all gathered on the far side of the wagons from the ridge, Arch asked: "Could anybody find their way in daylight to the fort?"

Joe Debson said: "Yeah. I reckon."

"All right, Joe. You break out with us. When we're clear, you can dust for the fort. Get the soldiers. You seen everythin' that's happened here an' you tell 'em."

Joe asked: "Where shall the soldiers go?"

"Here. That'll give 'em a start."

He whistled shrilly and called Ben Goodall.

198

In a minute or two Ben appeared out of the darkness. Arch asked him: "You know where the men over there're at?"

"There's a small hill," Ben said, "about two hundred yards directly due west of here. My guess is they're on top. There's maybe two, three of 'em."

"Good. Mount up all of you."

It was a chore getting the wounded on the mules. But there were no complaints from the injured men. Two of them were so weak that they had to have their ankles tied under the bellies of their animals. Arch heaved Martha up onto a mule. They had made a rough saddle for her out of harness straps and blankets. For stirrups, she had part of a rawhide lariat. Her rifle was tied under her left leg. A revolver was tucked into a man's belt around her slender waist. When she was up, Arch patted her thigh encouragingly.

"Don't stop for nothin', honey," he said. He raised his voice slightly. "Don't nobody stop for nothin'. We have to get as many people away as possible. Stick together and keep goin'. Now, you hear me. Nobody stops for nothin'."

They grunted a reply. They didn't like it much, he could tell.

He walked to his own mule. He had managed to recover his saddle from the dead bay under cover of darkness. He would need it. He had plenty to do. He swung up.

"I'm goin' north a ways," he said. "Charlie leads the way. I'll fire three shots quickly an' that means you fog it outa here. I'll catch you in minutes."

Martha protested as he knew she would.

"I'm not going without you, Arch." That was definite and flat.

Arch said: "Ben, you keep close to Martha. See she keeps goin'. See you soon."

He turned the mule into the darkness and heard Martha say sharply: "Arch Kelso, you just come back here. Ben, leave me go."

He quickened the pace of the mule with a touch of the spurs. The animal didn't like it much and tried pitching a little. Somebody up on the ridge started to fire a rifle. He kicked the mule into a run. It hit an awkward hurrying pace that at once tried to shake the guts out of him. He hadn't gone twenty paces when rifles started up in the west. That was good. That was what he wanted. They thought somebody was getting away for help.

He went on for a hundred yards or so and

swerved to the left, judging that would bring him to the north slope of the hill on which the attackers were stationed.

For a moment, their shooting had died away, but now, as he drew nearer to the hill, it opened up again. He kept the mule going, heading directly west. He was making so much noise that there was no possibility of knowing if the men up there were getting on the move. Certainly as he got past them, the shooting stopped once more. He heaved the rifle from its boot and triggered off three shots, praying that the men had orders to run down anybody trying to get clear. He raced on for a couple of hundred yards, leaving it to the mule to find safe running.

Then he pulled the animal to a halt and listened. There was no doubt about it. The men were getting their horses on the move and making a noise about it. He waited long enough to hear them piling down off the hill. At the same time, he heard the mules of the train get going. He wondered whether the men from the hill would turn toward them. He turned in the saddle and fired several shots back toward the hill. One of the men was shouting. He set off again, not changing his course. There was a chance that the men behind him had not heard the noise made by Martha and the men from the wagons.

There came a distant clatter of rifle fire. That would be the men on the ridge and those who had crossed the trail shooting at the wagon crew. He slowed his pace to give the men behind him time to come nearer. He knew that he was taking a risk, but it had to be taken.

Suddenly, he was in clear moonlight. It came as a shock. One moment, he was protected by a comforting darkness, the next it seemed as bright as daylight and he felt naked. He looked back and saw the flitting dark shapes behind him and knew they had seen him. He used the spurs and the mule jumped forward.

He broke from the rough and came abruptly onto a flat part of the plain and cursed. He wanted cover. He swung half-right and knew that would give his pursuers the opportunity to take a short cut. He glanced back again and saw that they were uncomfortably close.

They mustn't get him, he told himself. Everything rested on him staying alive, the recovery of the gold, Martha, the men and their survival.

He became conscious of brush tearing at him

and the mule and saw that he was in the rough again, smashing his way through brush. This was his chance. He brought the mule to a slithering halt, piled from the saddle and started shooting.

It seemed that he had no sooner pressed the trigger than the men were stopped and getting out of the saddle. He saw the horses running loose. Lead hummed viciously around him. The mule gave a rough cough that turned into a peculiar moaning note. He continued his firing, knowing that he had little chance of hitting anything in the uncertain light. He heard the sound of a heavy body falling and knew that the mule was down. He swore insanely. This meant that he was finished. Afoot.

But as suddenly as he was finished, he had hope.

A loose horse clattered near.

His rifle clicked harmlessly and he knew that it was empty.

The loose horse was off to his right, crashing through the brush. It stopped, no doubt brought to a halt by a trailing line.

He started running, keeping low.

A man shouted.

He tripped on something, went down and got

himself on his feet again. Before he recovered himself, he heard a horse neigh almost in his face and nearly ran into the animal. He reached out a hand for it and it shied away from him.

"Goddam you, you bastard," he said.

The horse stumbled on its line. Arch caught it by the mane and it jumped forward, ripping him from his feet. He was hampered by the rifle in his left hand, but he wasn't going to be parted from that. He got his feet under him again, not letting go of the mane and vaulted into the saddle. The horse started pitching and nearly went down as it trod on the trailing line. Arch transferred the rifle to his right hand, reached forward for the line and found it. Groping for the line tied around the saddlehorn, he freed it and kicked the horse with his spurred heels, not waiting to get his feet in the irons. The horse pitched a couple of times and he used the spurs again, savagely, swearing like a maniac. The horse got it into its head that he was boss and lit out. Arch got his feet into the stirrup-irons and rode.

He turned directly west again, keeping as fast a pace as the animal could hold for a quarter-mile, then angled left. Five minutes later, he halted and listened. The crashing flight of several animals reached his ears and he got the horse on the move again.

A few minutes later, he saw the dark mass that was a bunch of riders and hoped to God that he had found the right one. He curved in toward them, shouting.

A cry came back and he knew that Martha had made it. A moment later he was by her side and he was a part of the bunch racing recklessly through the night. They held a good pace for another mile and he called a halt. They all listened and Ben Goodall said: "We left 'em."

The animals blew.

"All right," Arch said. "By my reckoning, Joe, you ought to head north-west from here to hit the fort. Off with you."

"Here I go, fellers," said Joe. He was a little scared and showed it.

They wished him luck and he rode off into the moonlight, hoping he didn't meet bushwhackers or Indians. They went on. The wounded were suffering, but they made no complaint and Arch steeled himself to keep the pace. The sooner they were in Tucson, the sooner they were safe from the danger of Apache; the sooner they were in Tucson, the sooner they would be comparatively safe from the men who had raided the train. Arch couldn't be sure that they would not take up the trail of the refugees as soon as it was daylight. One of the most important parts of their plan must be to prevent news of their raid to get to the outside world.

Dawn found the hardy mules still heading roughly south at a hammering trot that must have been pure torture to the wounded. It was plain hell on the riders used to the easier pace of a horse. The light did not reveal to Arch any features of the country that he knew, but he had gambled on hitting the Tucson road again. He consulted the others and George Mathers reckoned they were heading for the road all right. His estimate was that they would reach it in the next few miles. Charlie Garth agreed with this.

Sure enough they came on the road in the next half-hour. Arch experienced an enormous feeling of relief. The wounded could not take much more of this and Martha looked completely bushed.

They halted.

The mules stood wearily. Arch's horse had its head down. It had run almost to its limit. He looked around at the men and the one woman. The wounded drooped in the saddle, the others looked drawn and tired.

"I think you'll be pretty safe from here on," Arch said.

Martha jerked her head around and stared at him roundeyed.

"Why'd you say 'you'?" she demanded. Trust her not to miss a trick.

"I was hired to move that gold to Tucson," he said. "That's what I'm goin' to do."

It sounded like a little hero talking and he hated himself for it.

"You are *not*," she told him. "Get that fool idea out of your head. You're coming into town like the rest of us."

Ben said: "Not the rest of us. Arch'll need some help."

Martha curled her lip at him.

"And what do you think two men can do against a bunch like that? And if you do get the gold away from them, how do two men drive all those wagons? Can you tell me that?"

Ben smiled wryly.

"No, I can't, ma'am," he said. "But that's what we aim to do."

Charlie Garth said in his growling voice: "Three men could just about do it."

Something started to sing inside Arch. Hope rose like a bright sun-rise.

George Mather said: "Four could do it easy."

Arch laughed outright from sheer astonishment and elation.

"We stop right there," he said. "Four is all we need."

Ike Shoesmith said: "Hell, Arch, you need every gun you can muster. Nobody ain't stoppin' me sidin' you."

Arch went all soft inside so that he felt ashamed of himself.

"No, Ike," he said. "Martha and the wounded want protection into town. The rest of you head on in. We won't have no argument about it." Ike had a wife and three kids. He was one who had to come out of this alive. He looked angry now and started to protest. Arch shouted him down. Martha tried shouting Arch down, but he showed that he couldn't be moved.

She tried reason.

"Just come on into town," she said. "You won't get far on a horse like that. You need fresh animals."

"That'd lose time," he said. "Besides there's plenty of fresh stock back there north of the train. Them fellers won't catch all of 'em up."

He climbed down and took the saddle off the horse. It wasn't a bad fit for him and he hankered riding back there on a good saddle. "I'll take your mule, Martha. This old horse'll get you into town fine and dandy."

She protested, but she climbed down and he put her homemade rig onto the horse and slapped his saddle on her mule. Compared to the other animals, this one was pretty fresh. Martha was light. So he put her up on the horse, patted her rump and said: "Joe's gone for the army. You head for Sheriff Styver when you hit town, honey. Tell him I reckon the men who took the train will head directly south for the border. If he travels east from Tucson, he ought to cut their sign. If it don't rain."

They looked at the sky, but it was clear without a wisp of cloud in it.

Martha's lip was trembling.

Softly, so only he could hear, she said: "I don't want you to go, Arch."

He looked up at her. "I have to, honey. You know that."

"I know," she admitted and patted his hand. He saw that there were tears in her eyes. He turned away and climbed on the mule. "Go on," he said. "An', Ike—don't stop for nothin'."

Ike lifted a hand. The little cavalcade moved on. Once Martha turned and waved. The four of them waved back, they turned their animals and moved along the road toward the north.

15

DOC started to his feet when he heard the sudden rush of movement and the pounding of hoofs from below. A few minutes before, a solitary rider had ridden west and he thought that his men over there would stop him. But this was a general exodus and the meaning of that and what it could entail filled him with a violent rush of panic.

With the panic came the realisation that the gold below was unguarded and the thought of the wealth that lay almost under his hand was almost too much for him. He gave a great shout and went stumbling and sliding down the trail side of the ridge.

Guns started up in the west. The men further up the trail were shooting, too. Near the wagons, he might run into the fire from his own men, but the thought never entered his head. The only thing he was conscious of was the overwhelming desire to see the gold.

Maybe the men on the ridge with him had the same thought. They came yelling after him.

One of them went down and howled his anger. Doc ran on oblivious of everything but the thought of the gold.

Suddenly, a wagon loomed up in front of him and, as he dodged clumsily around the rear of it, some sense of danger came to him. There might still be some men left with the wagons. He came around to the side of the wagon and halted, bawling for them to come out of cover or he'd kill the lot of them. He heard nothing but the sound of the retreating riders, the distant slamming of rifles and the pounding feet of his own men. As they came up, he shouted: "Check the wagons. Make sure there ain't nobody here."

He leaned his rifle against a wheel and started for the rear of a wagon, hauling himself, panting and wheezing over the tailboard, clutching at the crates with his hands. They were heavy. He started dragging one to the tailboard, sweating and cursing.

He heard the rip and splinter of wood from below.

A man yelled: "Christ, look at it."

There was silence.

Doc vaulted over the tailboard and a man struck a match.

"Put that light out," he snarled.

They ignored him. They stood and stared at the yellow stuff they had all killed men for. He joined them, fascinated for a moment into stillness. The match went out. The two men from the trail joined them. Another match was struck and once again they all stared as though they could never look their fill. Doc was so excited that he felt that he would vomit at any minute. He walked away a few paces to contain himself, to stop the terrible and consuming surge of emotion that had overtaken him, trying to possess himself once more. He listened. The flight of the train men was dying away. The firing had stopped.

He realised with a mild surprise that the moon was up and he could see quite clearly.

Taking out a cigar, he lit it and tried to think.

He was here in the middle of the desert with an emperor's ransom. He had the wagons and the men, but the teams had been scattered. That made him rage a little, but he suppressed the bitter anger against the men who had done this to him and tried to think his way out of this. He walked from wagon to wagon, assessing the gold in the crates, finding more thrown up as a barricade around the vehicles. There was more gold here than he had ever dreamed of, more than any mortal man could ever dream of. This could buy him anything on the face of the earth—power, respectability. He saw himself for a moment, powerful and respectable, drinking and eating the best, living like a king, beautiful women around him. For a moment, the possibilities seemed so close to him that he felt physically weak.

The chatter of the men seemed unreal and distant.

But he must think. Everything depended on him.

He had spare mules on the other side of the ridge. He could load up every one of them and take a fortune out of here. But that wouldn't be a quarter of the gold on the wagons. If he used the pack mules, he could maybe move quicker and through rougher country than if he used the wagons, but it meant leaving a hell of a lot of gold behind. There was a gamble even by using pack mules. Those bastards that had got away could warn the law, the military. At top speed and no snags it would take him several days to reach the border, pushing hard and travelling night and day. With the wagons it could take longer.

Should he catch up the scattered mules and risk the slow way with the wagons, hurry straight for the border with a pack-train or, and this might be the smartest move, go east into the hills with a pack train made up of his own mules and the train's mules? He could lose pursuit more easily in the hills. He could cross the border under cover of the mountains. That seemed a good bet. He reckoned he'd give that a whirl. See what mules he could catch in the dawn and after plan from there. He'd decide his moves as opportunities arose. What man could ever know what the next day would bring? The next hour?

Joe Price was standing near, lovingly handling a bar of gold.

"Joe," he said quietly to the 'breed, "go get the animals. Yance, give him a hand. Dirk, are all the boys here?"

Dirk started counting heads. He came back to say that they were all there. Doc set his guards, putting men on the ridges and others on the edge of camp. He gave orders for the rest to sleep, but they were too excited to do so. Doc took a small flask of whiskey from a pocket and took a healthy swig. That settled his churning guts a little. He told one of the men

215

to find him something to eat and a few minutes later was sitting on a crate of gold, eating cold bacon and beans and washing them down with bitter water. He started to do arithmetic, trying to work out how long it would take Kelso to fetch either the soldiers from the fort or the law from Tucson. The army might come, probably would on the double, but he doubted if the law would willingly come out of Tucson with the Indian scare as it was. He dozed as he sat there and suddenly it seemed, it was dawn.

Rising stiffly to his feet, he stretched and yawned. He lighted his first cigar of the day and dragged smoke into his lungs with relish. A man sat near him, awake with a rifle across his knees. A half-dozen blanket-draped men lay prone, asleep. Doc started kicking them awake and they lifted their heads, cursing. They stopped when they saw it was him. Nobody ever cursed Doc and got away with it, not even tough gun-hands like them. They got to their feet, looking gray-faced and wretched in the cold light of the dawn. Doc told them to throw their hulls on their horses and get after the scattered teams. If they wanted the gold, they wouldn't get an ounce of it without the animals. One wanted coffee before he rode and Doc

216

turned on him, spitting like an enraged mountain lion and the man hurried away to obey him. He watched them catch up their horses and saddle. He put Dirk in charge of them, telling him they didn't have all the time in the world. Dirk nodded and rode off north with the men behind him.

Doc started worrying then about having the wagons of gold and no more than three men to guard them. He tramped to the top of the nearest ridge where Joe Price stood watch. He could see from a bulge in the 'breed's pocket that Joe had at least one bar of gold on him. Doc didn't blame him.

Joe said: "They gone to ketch up the teams?"

"Yeah."

Joe grinned briefly. He could add two and two together.

"You don't aim to leave none of this behind."

Doc pulled on his cigar. "I don't know yet," he said. He felt the need to confide in another human, a need that came rarely to him. "We'll see how the cards fall. Time is the important thing. We can't wait for ever for the mules to come in. We have to move. It was my plan that nobody would leave this train alive. They did.

Anythin' can happen now. The soldiers could come after us. The law. We have to move fast."

"You takin' the wagons?"

"I told you. I don't know." He nodded toward the dust raised by the departed riders. "See how many animals they bring in. We could pack the gold into the hills. Safer than headin' straight for the border. Everybody'll expect us to head that a-way."

Joe nodded.

"That could be smart. You thought of Juanito?"

Doc looked somber.

"I ain't never stopped thinkin' of the bastard. But I don't know as I'm afraid of that one. We got some boys with us is awful handy with a gun. I reckon we could see them Indians off."

Joe said. "The army didn't do so good at that."

With derision, Doc snorted: "The army!"

"And there's Kelso," Joe said. "I know Kelso. Them fellers buried their dead, but I'm bettin' Kelso wasn't among 'em. Kelso's headed for Tucson right now. That could mean anythin'."

"I ain't forgotten Kelso either," Doc said.

"So the hills could be a good way to head," Joe said.

Doc nodded and walked down the ridge-side. He felt better for the few words exchanged with the halfbreed.

Back at the wagons he set to work, cutting the canvas covers of the wagons to make pouches for the gold. He had made up his mind. He would pack the gold into the hills. And he felt even better for having made up his mind. A kind of small sub-plan came into his mind, an extension of the bigger one. A small plan that applied only to himself and excluded the other men. The thought of it made him smile to himself. He decided that nobody in the train knew he was leading the attack. That being so, this second plan was a pretty good idea. When his men got hold of the gold, the gold would get hold of them. Anything could happen after that. But he wouldn't be a part of it.

He smiled gently to himself and fired a second cigar. He would have to go carefully with them for a while; he did not have too many left. He called Witt from the hillock to the west and got him to give a hand making the pouches. They cut them with their knives and fastened the sides with pieces of rope cut from the wagons. They had a good many made by the time the riders returned from the north. It was near noon and by this time Doc was almost beside himself with anxiety. By this time, he knew, Kelso would have been able to reach Tucson. By now the law and the army could have been alerted. Doc knew that he would have to be deep in the hills pretty soon to be even slightly safe. Then he would have to start worrying about the Indians. But first things first; one thing at a time.

He got the men working. They wanted to eat, but he lashed them with his tongue. They sweated in the heat as they loaded the gold into the pouches. As soon as they were filled they were slung on mules. Doc counted. Adding the additions to his own, he had about thirty and thirty mules could carry a lot of gold. He wondered how many he could get away with for his own and private use. One thing he knew for sure: he would not desert his men till he was safe out of Juanito's reach. He had a profound respect for the cunning and ferocity of that Indian. It just about equalled his own. He could give higher praise to no man.

Doc was so urgent to depart from that spot

that he worked side by side with the men and that was something he had not done for many a year. He liked to stride around and goad other men to fresh effort with his tongue. He was quite inspired with his tongue, was Doc.

He was glad to see that everybody worked with a will. They had plenty of reason. They weren't too afraid of the law. Their concerted guns could cause any ill-assorted and hastily raised posse to turn tail, but they had some respect for the army. Not that the army was in itself in this instance any more formidable than a posse. Maybe even less, for those soldier boys weren't exactly expert with their firearms. But fighting the army on one day could bring a great deal of trouble to a man on a later one. No, it was better not to tangle with Uncle Sam. Better by far to be one jump ahead and safely in the hills. So the men worked hard and fast, spurred on to extra effort by the thought that their future was in their own hands. If they could get away with this little lot, their cut-throat and hand-to-mouth days were over. They worked more willingly than they had ever done before in their lives, sweating in the sun, fevered and driven by their dreams.

By noon or shortly thereafter the last mule

was packed and the guards called in. They came on the run. Every man was loaded with all the water he could carry, for nobody knew when next they would come on any. They found corn for the animals in the wagons and every saddle-mule and pack-mule and horse was given a sack-load to carry. If the animals weren't kept in good condition, they might as well not start their trip.

As they filed past him across the road and up the ridge beyond, Doc was tempted to set fire to the deserted wagons. He did not know why, but the instinct was there, as if he wanted to see blotted out the last sign of the men who had defied him and, in a small way, defeated him. But he refrained. The smoke might lead the law or the soldiers to the spot the quicker. He shoved his rifle away into the boot under his leg and urged his horse after his departing cohorts. As he went down off the ridge, he chuckled to himself. He had the feeling that he was going to get away with this. When the wagon-train people had managed to get away under cover of dark, he had thought it might be all up with him, but he felt better now. He started to hum. By God, he felt gay.

16

BY the time they got near the train or
where they thought they had left it, men
and animals were tired through to their
bones. Arch felt that he had not slept for a
week. Some of his mind was back there with
Martha, hoping that by now she was safely in
Tucson. It was lucky that the attackers had
made their try so close to town. This way, there
was just a chance that shortly there might be
some help coming up behind.

When they were within what they thought to
be a couple of miles of the spot where the
wagons were, George went forward to scout.
The others dismounted and rested the animals,
easing the cinches if there were any to ease. The
only shade the men could find was that thrown
by the animals. They lay in these small patches
and thought of crystal clear water and cold beer.

They would have been tense if they had not
been so tired. If they had seen Juanito and his
band of renegades come around the bend of the
trail they would have stared at him phlegmatic-

ally before putting their rifles to their shoulders. They were as emotionally as physically exhausted and the human emotions have their limits.

It didn't take George long. Pretty soon, he came trotting back on a very tired mule. He halted about a quarter mile from them and beckoned them on. As they urged their animals forward, Arch said: "Keep your eyes skinned, boys. Maybe we've run right into real trouble."

They reached George and he told them: "Wagons're around the bend. Most of the gold's gone. Well, a hell of a lot of it."

Arch said: "We'll go around. Ben, you come in from the east. You smell trouble there, you fire your rifle and come arunnin'."

Ben nodded and set off. Arch led the others off the road to the west and skirted the ridge in much the same way as he had when he had nearly ridden into the attackers. They had their rifles out when they came within sight of the wagons. The whole scene looked still and quiet. Arch sensed that if there was danger, it might come from further west. That would be the unexpected direction. He kept turning his eyes that way as he rode in. Ben Goodall appeared on the further ridge and waved to them before he sent his mule down onto the road. They met up at the wagons.

"George," said Arch, "get up on the highest point you can find and keep watch."

George rode off, going south.

The others walked around the wagons, peering in them. Arch saw there was a good deal of gold there. He reckoned that the raiders had not taken anywhere near half. So he had an additional problem on his hands. He not only had to find a way of getting back the missing gold, but he had to safeguard that which remained. He didn't know the answer to that one.

There was food and water in the wagons. The raiders had slipped. They should have destroyed that.

He sat down in the shade of a wagon and smoked a pipe, thinking. The others prepared a meal, lit a fire and made coffee. They weren't in a mood to worry about who saw the smoke. If Juanito was anywhere around, he knew they were there by now.

He walked around and read sign. There was an awful jumble and mess of it and he could not make much of it beyond the fact that a number of men and animals had walked around here. He went north up the trail and reckoned that the attackers had been after the remuda and the mules they had cut loose from the wagons and scattered. He wondered if any animals had been left free. Should he try to get the gold here into Tucson? No, there wasn't a chance of doing that. He didn't have the men even if he could muster the teams.

So he had to make this gold safe and go after the rest.

How make it safe?

Only one answer to that—bury it. Right there in the middle of camp and walk the mules over the spot where it was buried.

He walked back to the wagons and told the men: "We bury the gold."

They groaned just as he knew they would. But they fetched picks and shovels from the wagons and started digging. Arch joined them and they sweated hard in the sun. His only comfort was that all this time, the mules were resting and eating their heads off. As he ripped up the hard virgin earth, he thought about the fact that he was burying the gold right alongside Mel. That took his thoughts along the obvious road to how many men had died because of that same gold. He rested for a moment on his pick and thought. How many more men would die before he got it to Tucson?

He was a man grown and he had learned his first real lesson; just like a kid needed to learn a lesson. He had taken on this job so that he could make himself a stake, so that he could buy himself and Martha something of a future together. None of it was worth men's lives and the sorrow of their women and children. Life was cheap on the frontier, but not that cheap. Now he was in this up to his neck, he would have to go through with it. He had given his word to the mine-owners and a man's word still meant something in this country; his whole reputation rested on it. But when he was done, he would think twice before his profit had come out of the death of a man.

He spat on his hands and went on hacking away at the hard surface of the earth.

When he thought that the trench was deep enough and big enough, he told Ben and George to ride north and see if they could pick up the sign of any of the mules. Sure, he knew their attackers had gone after them, but it was his bet that they had been in a hurry and had missed some. The four of them needed fresh mounts like nobody's business. He told them to look out for Indians, but he knew that he was telling them what they already knew. He watched them depart with doubt weighing heavily on him, watched them fade away into the pale dust of distance, but knowing that he had to have fresh saddle-stock or the four of them might find their end in this kind of country. He decided he didn't like being a leader of men. A man had to be callous for that and Arch could never make himself that. He had a soft streak in him and he guessed he'd never be rid of it. Take Ben Goodall now—he was a different kind of animal. Since his wife and kids had been killed, he had walked and talked like a man and even laughed at times, but he killed like an animal, without regret. Maybe one day, he would grow out of it, maybe something would happen that would bring back the humanity to him, but he would be a long while yet.

Arch turned back to Charlie and said: "Right, let's get this gold underground."

Charlie grunted: "We don't have anybody lookin' over the country now."

Arch growled: "We don't have time for niceties."

They dragged the heavy crates and dumped

228

them in the trench. It was hot, back-breaking work in the sun, but, in the middle of the afternoon, they were done. They scooped the earth back on the crates, patted it down and walked the mules back and forth over it, giving the gold the same funeral that their dead had had. The thought sobered them, if their thoughts weren't sober enough already.

Charlie asked: "What about the wagons?"

"Leave 'em. Who knows? Luck might just be with us and they might be here when we get back."

Arch filled his pipe, fired it and walked to the top of the ridge to look out over the country. He was getting anxious about Ben and George. He knew if they were mule hunting, they might not be back till the following day, but he was anxious just the same. He saw a long line of dust far to the west and watched it through his glass, but he couldn't make head nor tail of it except that there must have been a good many horses there and whoever it was was headed north-east. That meant that they could meet up with Ben and George. That started him worrying some more. He told himself that it wouldn't do anybody any good, but he worried just the same.

He put the glass on the hills and spent a good while checking them over. Nothing moved. The pastel yellows, pinks and blues hurled back the sun's glare at him, the mountains squatted massively and in forbidding silence. Pretty soon, if all went well he would be in among their folds after the gold, a chin on either shoulder for fear of Indians and bandits, more like the hunted than a hunter. For a moment, the thought came to him that he was crazy to make this try with no more than four men. If he met up with Indians, he was finished. Why, a whole army hadn't been able to corral Juanito. What could four men do if they faced him?

He thought he saw a wisp of dust on the trail to the north. He put his glass on it and thought it looked like a good many animals moving in this direction. His hopes rose.

It could have been his imagination, but he thought he saw two specks that could have been riders. He whistled Charlie and pointed to the north. When he looked through the glass again, the moving dots were closer and he tried to convince himself that they were mules being driven.

He looked into the west and the long line of dust had disappeared. He ran the glass back and forth, but he couldn't pick up a trace of the fast-moving line. The dust on the road came steadily ahead. He ran down the ridge and called to Charlie: "It's the boys, I guess, with the mules. Let's go meet them."

Charlie reckoned that was a good idea. He saddled his mule and swung up.

"You sure it's them?" he asked.

"No, I ain't sure."

"Then we'll go mighty careful."

They trotted out onto the road. It wasn't long before they saw it was Ben and George. The sight of them would have been enough to cheer Arch, but the animals they brought with them was an even better tonic. Ahead of them they drove four mules and two horses. Arch was so damned pleased, he laughed outright.

"Toss you boys for a horse. My crotch don't fancy no more mule," he shouted.

George and Ben were tired, but they were all smiles. The four of them drove the animals to the wagons and stepped down. Arch rubbed his hands. The animals looked in good condition. They'd make good speed with them.

"I saw dust yonder to the west," he said.

"Yeah," Ben said, "we did too. We didn't

see what made it. Could of been army, could have been Indians."

George pulled a long face.

"I'm crazy," he remarked carelessly. "I could of gone ahead to town and I could have my guts full of booze and my arms full of woman. But I have to come out here where I can lose my hair."

Ben grinned his quick nervous grin.

"Apaches don't take hair," he said. "They take somethin' more important to a man."

George scowled.

"If'n you'd of told me that sooner, I'm damn sure I wouldn't of come."

Arch got them to work. They put saddles and what passed for saddles on fresh horses and mules, packed water, supplies, feed for the animals and ammunition on the other animals. Arch wondered if he should leave some of the mules behind, thinking they might slow the pace, but he decided against it. They might need spares and he was certain he would need the supplies and the ammunition. The pursuit not only relied on speed, but on survival.

"There ain't too much daylight left," he said, "but a couple of hours could tell. We all agree to move out now?"

They all agreed. They wanted to get on the move and finish the chore as soon as they could. Arch took the lead, guided the dun horse he rode up the ridge and headed into the hills.

He followed the plain sign till dark. The men who had robbed the train had made no attempt to hide their trail; they were in a hurry. Maybe they would try to confuse the pursuit later; maybe they thought there would be no pursuit. By the time Arch halted, the going was starting to get tough, the ground was starting to be rugged, but there was nothing that the animals could not negotiate. Arch reckoned that where the bandits could go he and his men could. He was tired, but he was hopeful. In the next couple of days, he would come up with the bushwhackers and he would do to them what they had done to him. He wondered if it came to it, if he would show any more mercy. They had killed some good men. Among them had been his friend and partner, Mel.

It was a strange feeling, not knowing the men he was after. He had glimpsed faces as the riders had charged down on the wagons, but had known none of them. His guess was that they were from Crewsville. Outlaws did not hang out in these hills, not now the Apache were hiding in them and raiding far and wide from them. It had to be men from the town. That being so it could be any one of a dozen men who had led the raiders. It could, and he had to smile bitterly as the thought came to him, even be the marshal, John Stratton, who had blasted his way to many a crooked dollar in his day.

Soon, Arch promised himself, he would know.

They didn't find water, but they had plenty with them. They made a dry camp. They watered the mules from the containers on the back of one mule and fed them. They didn't light a fire and one of them stood guard while the others got into their blankets.

Before they slept, Ben asked Arch: "You know where I reckon they're headed, Arch?"

"The Saddle."

"Wouldn't that be a laugh? Yeah, it makes sense. If you had that much gold, you'd head for the border. But you'd want to throw off pursuit fast. Them bastards can't move fast. The gold fixes that. Five gets you ten, they've been greedy an' they're carryin' more gold than they should. Them mules is weighed down. So they head north-east. They got to have water, so the Saddle's the obvious place. There's water there all year around. They fill up an' they scatter. Every man for himself."

Arch said: "Not while they're in Apache country."

"All right. So they put it off a little till later. But they'll scatter. By God, you know what? I reckon some of 'em'll head down into New Mexico."

Arch said: "If the Saddle's clear of Indians, I reckon they'll rest up a short while for the final haul. Them mules is going to be plumb tuckered out after this climb. Maybe we'll jump 'em there."

Ben sighed.

"Maybe," he said, longingly.

Charlie Garth's voice cut through the dark from Ben's other side.

"Five gets you ten, Juanito's sitting on that water like he was when you an' Mel went up there."

From where he stood on guard, George said: "Shut it, you fellers, you're frettin' me."

Arch rolled over, thought he would never get to sleep with the load he had on his mind and fell into a deep dreamless sleep.

17

DOC rode in the van of the winding column of men and animals, the head of his patient horse nodding before him. He knew that the horse was tired and that worried him. Not that he was sentimental about horses, but that meant that the mules, loaded down with gold as they were, would be even more tired. His mind turned this way and that, trying to plan, trying to think of every contingency, his eyes flicking over the country around him from under the shade of his hat.

The country was wild, as wild as any he had ever seen in his life and, as they went higher onto the Saddle, so the country turned greener. There was timber now, scattered to right and left; there ahead of him, he saw the first sign of green grass. That meant water and his heart lifted a little.

Ringus rode at his side, nervous, never taking his eyes from the rocks and trees, thinking he saw an Indian in every shadow.

"We left a trail a kid could follow," he said.

"Why a Goddam pilgrim could follow us up here, Doc." That showed how scared he was. He would never have dared to speak to his leader that way back in town. Doc merely grunted. But Ringus didn't notice the danger signs, his tongue took him on and on, complaining, whining.

Finally, Doc couldn't take much more of it.

"For Crissake," he said. "Quit bellyachin'. I know what I'm doin'. We can leave all the sign we want till we reach the Saddle. Then we split up. That's when we wipe out our sign."

Ringus stared at him, mouth wide.

"Split up?" he said and his voice went high-pitched. "Juanito's up here. Doc, you can't mean that." Doc looked at him and saw terror plain on his face.

"In twos an' threes," he said.

"That's a mite better," Ringus said. "My God, I ain't ridin' through no Indian country on my lonesome." He grinned hesitatingly. "Who you goin' to take with you, Doc."

Doc looked at him as a father would look at a son.

"Why you, Ringus," he told the other. "Who else?"

Ringus looked almost happy. Doc had chosen

him from all the others. He'd be safe with Doc who could look after himself anywhere.

The sound of the animals' hoofs changed as they left the hard trail for grass. The animals perked up and quickened their pace as if they knew already that water lay ahead of them. Doc halted and the animals started plucking at the grass. Doc called Witt Brand and Joe Price to him.

"Joe," he asked, "how far is the water from here, do you reckon?"

"One smoke," Joe told him.

"Witt," Doc said, "you an' Joe ride as far as the water an' look around. See if there's been any Apache around lately."

They both looked a little startled. The task was to neither's liking.

Joe said: "Maybe them Indians is there now."

"Maybe," Doc agreed. "Now get goin'."

They both looked like they wanted to argue, but they saw the look in Doc's eyes and they turned their horses and rode up the green sloping meadowland that led to the water. Doc gave orders for cinches to be loosened and for the mules to be kept close. He told them all to keep their eyes skinned. From here on if they were careless they could be dead and dead men couldn't spend gold. They lolled on the grass, sipped water from their canteens and smoked. There wasn't a lot of talking. The two wounded men lay flat and rested. The ride had been painful and exhausting to them. If the thought of their share of the gold had not been with them they would have opted out far back on the trail.

Within the hour Joe Price and Witt Brand returned. Joe said there was some old Apache sign around, but he reckoned that there hadn't been an Indian near the place in days. Doc seemed satisfied with that. He gave orders for cinches to be tightened and for them to move out. Slowly, the mule train and its guardians moved on its way.

After a while, the going got easier as the land leveled out as they got onto the Saddle itself. Suddenly, the grass was lusher and the trees greener. It didn't seem possible that there could be a spot like this in the heart of the arid hills. The animals were straining now to break into a trot. A few minutes later it was as much as the riders could do to hold them. Doc shouted hoarsely. They must all stay close. He didn't want anybody rushing in there. He yelled for two men to go ahead and take up positions in the rocks that he could now see on the other side of the water. Two of the Brand boys rode ahead. Doc watched them reach the water and dismount. The animals walked straight into the water and started to drink. Doc cursed, them Brand boys were born fools. The horses would foul up the water. He watched the two tall men clamber into the rocks. They looked around them, it seemed, before they waved back to the train. Doc allowed the pace to be quickened then.

Five minutes later, Doc gave orders for the men to build a fire. They would have hot coffee, by God, they had all earned it. After that, they sat around drinking coffee and talking about what they would do when they reached civilisation. Doc put a stop to it all when he said: "We camp here tonight and rest the animals. We stick together till noon tomorrow. Then we split up."

That caused some consternation. They all talked at once. Most of them didn't like the idea of splitting because they didn't know this country. There were most likely Indians about and they could get themselves lost in five minutes up here. No, they didn't like the idea of splitting up.

"By now," Doc told them, "the law or the army or both know the gold's been taken. It won't be so long before men're comin' into these hills for just one reason: to put us all behind bars. Then hang us. We stay together an' they catch us. We split, we have a chance."

Stet Brand said: "I don't like it, Doc. If we're caught in ones and twos we don't have a chance."

"This ain't the time for fightin'. That's what we'll have on our hands if we stay together—a big fight. This is the time for stayin' alive and reapin' some benefit from all this lovely gold. We do like I say—travel east from here tomorrow, divide and hide our trails."

"It'll take us a hell of a time to get out of these hills," Dirk said. "We don't have supplies for that time."

Doc snapped: "If you go careful, you all have enough for a week. You have guns, you can shoot things, can't you? There'll be water a-plenty on the New Mexican side. Christ, you can live on the country for a bit, can't you?"

A man named Morgan, bleary-eyed and

groggy from travel, said: "None of us don't like it, Doc. That's straight."

Doc's patience was thin. He was tired, he wanted to head on with his gold.

"I got you the gold, didn't I?" he shouted. "What more do you want? Do I have to hold your Goddam hands for the rest of the trip?"

The men looked sour. Ringus squatted by the fire, poking the wood with a stick, looking distressed. He liked the idea of staying with Doc, but he would have liked the company of others until he was clear of these hills.

Witt Brand turned his head and looked at the rocks.

He yelled inarticulately, pointing.

They all swung around, staring.

Rod Brand was acting strangely, stepping off a rock into the air. He disappeared into the jumble of rocks below and they heard him hit. It was a horrible sound combining the pounding of flesh and the breaking of bones.

Witt heaved a gun from leather and started running. Stet Brand came running out of the rocks, his eyes wild and his face chalky.

"Indians!" he screamed.

For a moment, every man there had stayed still, chilled to immobility. But now they moved. They were fighting men by profession and combat was to them an instinct. Each man swooped for his rifle.

Doc's first thought was for the gold.

"Ringus, the mules."

A large-bore gun boomed in the rocks. Stet threw up his arms and slithered along the ground on his face. A man or two threw rifles to shoulder, searching for a target. Another ran to help Ringus with the mules. The animals were jumbled together near the water. They were pretty full of water and tired. They bunched fairly well now.

There was a rattle of shots from the rocks.

The mules tried to break now and Doc ran among them, catching up lines and yelling frantically to the men to hold them.

The men were firing into the rocks now. The shooting there died away.

Doc was shouting for them to get the mules away from the rocks and into the open. The men ran to their horses, piled into the saddle and started to drive the pack-train quickly and untidily into the wide open space that approached the water and the rocks beyond. Doc threw anxious glances behind him, saw nothing and galloped after them.

243

In the dead center of the grassy meadow, Doc called a halt. He had decided what he would do. There was going to be danger from civilisation maybe the following day. But the danger right now was from Indians. And he didn't doubt that it was Apache who had shot at them from the rocks. Dark was on them now and there would be no escape from here in the dark. The Indians if they were going to attack again, would do so in the dawn. So he had to win a fight at dawn from good cover and get out of here then.

At his orders, the men staked the animals close and made up a rough barricade of the gold packs and the rest of the gear. They had a couple of shovels with them and threw up some additional earthworks. This didn't amount to much, for the men hated manual labor, but it was better than nothing.

That done, they settled down and Doc talked to them, checking how much the men had seen of the attackers. Two of them swore that they had seen Indians plainly. That confirmed what Doc already believed and he was satisfied. His main anxiety now was the mules and horses. In the center of the little fortress they were highly vulnerable and he could not afford to lose any of them. He set a guard, detailed the men who were to take second watch, rolled in a blanket and tried to get to sleep.

Sleep came to him reluctantly and late. His mind would not stop trying to think of a way out for him personally. It did not matter to him what happened to these others. He wanted to get out with as much gold as possible. Several times, he was tempted to break out of here in the dark with a pack-mule and chance his luck, but he knew the idea was crazy and he wouldn't get far. If his own men didn't kill him, the Indians would.

No, from here on, he must live for the moment, ever watchful of an opportunity of making his escape both from his friends and his enemies.

18

SOMEBODY was shaking him roughly. Doc opened his eyes and saw that it was still dark.

Near his right ear a man whispered: "It's time." Memory flooded back to him. He had told the last watch that he must be roused before dawn. He threw off the blanket and shivered in the chill air. Standing up, he stretched and scratched. He was stiff and he could have done with hot coffee. It was painful, the way he yearned for coffee. He reached for his flask and took a nip. That warmed him a little.

He could see the dim shapes of the men moving inside the barricade. They made little noise. But the mules were stirring and if there were any Indians around the location of the camp would be evident to them from the sounds.

He went around, checking that every man was in position, that every one of them had ample ammunition. It would not be long before they were levering and triggering as fast as they could move and ammunition would be burned away fast.

Ringus asked in a shaking voice: "Are they goin' to attack us, Doc?"

Doc snarled: "How in hell should I know."

He settled himself down with his rifle. It rested on a large pouch of gold. The close proximity of the precious metal put heart into him. The first cold finger of dawn pointed across the night sky to a new day. A lobo howled. The sound was close and it sent a chill down Doc's spine. He could face any whiteman on earth with a gun, but Apaches he didn't swallow so well. They could do such fancy things to a man.

The light started to spread. Slowly, Doc's vision lengthened. One of the horses trumpeted and an animal fought to pull up its stake.

"This'll be it, boys," Doc said over his shoulder and they all heard him.

If they didn't come now, they wouldn't come at all.

It was nearly daylight. Doc began breathing heavily, realising that he had been holding his breath. Maybe it was too late. They wouldn't come now.

A mule coughed, the cough turned to a wheezing scream. Doc glanced hastily over his shoulder and saw an animal near him go down. The others shied away from him.

A gun boomed.

Doc switched his attention to the front and saw the figures seemingly come out of the ground, close.

There was scarcely time to elevate his rifle and fire. But he was shaken, filled with a sudden panic and he missed. A yell split the morning air, rifles went off all around him and a running figure was almost on top of him. Doc knew that he was at a complete disadvantage if he stayed where he was flat on the ground. He tried heaving his bulk to his feet, levering his rifle as he moved and fired point-blank.

The heavy slug hit the man in mid-air as he made his leap over the barricade. He landed on Doc and his flying weight carried him violently to the ground. He fell among the animals. They were lashing out wildly with their hoofs. Something struck him in the side as he scrambled clear and he was flung across the ground, yelling.

He was on his hands and knees, his rifle gone. The din around him was deafening, the explosion of guns mixed with the noise of the animals and the shouts of men.

As he staggered to his feet, there was a sudden rush of movement in front of him. Ringus rose into his line of vision and he thought he heard the man scream. A dim form was stabbing away repeatedly at Ringus who seemed to fall away from it limp and soft like an old rag. He hit the ground without sound.

Doc had his Colt's gun in his hand, thumbing back the hammer. The Indian turned quickly toward him, first crouched, then springing. Doc fired from the hip, but he never knew if he made a hit. There was an animal stench in his nostrils and he was staggering back before the Indian's charge, going back into the jumping animals, smashing at the painted face in front of him with the barrel of his gun. The man lashed at him with a blade and Doc didn't know whether the steel had penetrated him or not. He had his teeth clenched tight as he battered away with the gun. Yet the blows seemed to have no effect, as if they were both dream figures in a nightmare. Fingers were on Doc's throat and that was no dream. He felt his breath cut off and he started to choke.

Doc was a physically powerful man. He went to hit with the gun, but it was gone. He brought his two hands up sharply inside the arms of his attacker and tore the lethal fingers from his throat. Then his own were clamped on that of his adversary. He saw the Indian's eyes widen. The Indian tried to knee him in the groin, but he blocked the attempt with his knees. He tightened his fingers around the brown throat. The man twisted violently and Doc's fingers slipped on the greased skin. When the man had nearly succeeded in getting himself free, Doc released him, kicked his feet from under him and smashed a hamlike fist in his face, driving him backward. Doc followed in a fury of fear and destruction, kicking savagely at the man as he tried wretchedly to rise. Somebody cannoned into Doc at that moment and nearly knocked him from his feet. He was carried away from the Indian, weaponless in the middle of a fight.

Near him he saw the back of an Indian's tangled head, red rag showing like a beacon, a spotted shirt shoved into soldiers pants that had the backside cut out of them. The savage was slashing at somebody Doc couldn't identify. Doc seized the Indian by the nape of his long hair and with a howl of ferocity and joy, ripped him from his feet and hurled him over the barricade. On the ground a gun caught his eye.

Stooping he picked it up and checked the loads. Three shots left.

The Indian he had hurled forth was on his feet making noises like a scalded puma, leaping back into the fight. Doc met him face to face and fired. The man jacknifed from the bullet in his belly and Doc blew his brains out as he went down.

He became aware that the noise had stopped.

He swung around.

A figure darted away across the grass. There, another. And another. Good God, the Apaches were running. He fired the last round in the pistol and knew that the range was too long.

"Fire," he yelled at his men. "Kill the bastards."

Not a shot came.

He looked around at them. Hardly a man stood on his feet. Near him Witt Brand was kneeling, his face black with powder, his eyes screwed up as if he were in pain, loading his rifle.

From somewhere in the little fortress a man groaned.

"Aw, Christ . . . Aw, Jesus Christ . . . right in the belly."

Joe Price was on his feet, blood streaming

251

down his face, thumbing bullets into his Remington pistol.

"So there ain't no Goddam Indians around here," Doc said affably.

"Honest, Doc, there wasn't no sign."

There were two mules down, one of them kicking. The others were scared and restless, but they were on their feet. The Indians would save them if they could, because most likely they needed them. Mules were good in Apache country. Doc had heard they even liked mule meat.

The Indians had disappeared now.

The flies buzzed hungrily at the blood.

"Somebody kill that damn mule," Doc said.

A man lay on his face to his left, sprawling, hands still in the position of clutching at a pouch of gold. That was Ringus. Doc went over to him, stooped and rolled him onto his back. The head moved loosely. It had almost been hacked from the body. Doc wasn't a squeamish man, but the sight turned his stomach a little. He pursed his lips.

Looking at the bloody remains, he thought: "Who else? Who else is dead? How many do I have left? Will there be enough to hold off the Indians?"

He straightened and walked around the circle.

It was Dirk Brand who had been stabbed in the belly. He was groaning and babbling wildly. Back in Crewsville he had a wife. Men said he was crazy about her.

Doc said: "Pull your knees up, man. Lie on your side and roll up in a kind of bunch or your guts'll come out." He'd seen it happen before now. That was after the Comanches had got through with a man out on the Staked Plains. A good few years back. He didn't think Dirk heard him.

Beyond Dirk was his brother Witt. He had a flesh wound in one arm and the knuckles of one hand had been slashed across by a knife. He went to move his brother as Doc had suggested. As he did so, he looked up at Doc and asked: "Is he finished?"

Doc nodded. "Sure."

The brothers were devoted to each other. He saw the dead, hopeless look on Witt's face. The rest were loading guns, looking grim.

Doc found a cup, mixed whiskey and water together and took a drink. He had a sour taste in his mouth as if he had drunk too much the night before and had slept little since. He loaded the gun in his hand, put it in his holster and looked for his rifle. He found it lying under the Indian he had killed. He heaved the dead body aside, cleaned the rifle and fully loaded it.

"You men," he said. "Clear the dead out of it." There were three Indian dead. He wondered how many more there were to come.

Joe Price said: "Yonder," and pointed.

They were mounted now, bunched near the water, more than a good rifle shot away. So they were definitely going to have another try.

"Let's get ready," Doc said. Witt was still fussing over his last living brother. Doc sharpened his tone. "Witt, pick up your rifle. We got a fight on our hands."

Witt didn't seem to hear him.

Doc crouched down, rifle in hand and felt numb, as if he couldn't credit that this was happening to him. To have taken the train, gotten away this far with the gold and now this . . . It was too much for a man to take in. But there must be some way out, there must be something he could do to get away with just one mule-pack of gold.

He said: "They don't have more'n one rush in 'em, boys. We cut 'em down an' we move on. We make it so hot for 'em they don't come near us no more."

There weren't many Indians left now. If this was Juanito's bunch, they had sure been whittled down.

They were on the move, trotting their many-colored horses away from the trees and out into the open, bright rag fluttered, the sun caught the barrel of a rifle. Across the grass came a shrill challenging cry. Doc wondered if the red devils would keep on coming till they were all dead. Juanito certainly had the reputation of being a man without fear, a man who was driven by nothing but a hatred of the whites, sworn to dedicate his life to their destruction. How, Doc asked himself, could you stop a man like that?

The Indians had their horses at a flat run now, scattering out and whooping across the open space, the ground shaking under the flying hoofs.

Doc began firing. The other rifles opened up. A horse went down. The rider landed, running and continued the charge.

19

IT was Ben who heard the shooting. He signed for the others to stop and they halted their horses. The animals began to munch on the grass.

Faintly, far off, Arch heard the popping of guns.

At once, he guessed it could mean only one thing. The raiders had run into Juanito at the water just as he, Ben and Mel had.

"Let's go," he said and spurred his horse. "Leave the packs." Dropping the lines, the others set off after him, urging their horses up the slight grade. The pack-animals ran with them for a short distance, then stopped.

They ran up the grade for maybe a mile with the sound of the guns getting louder as they neared the water. Arch was in the lead on his horse with the others streaming out behind him.

Suddenly, he saw movement and the dark wisps of smoke ahead and pulled in his horse. The others came up and the animals stood, blowing.

They could see the darting horsemen swooping in like hawks on the dark mass of animals in the center of the great sweep of grass. Distantly, there came the high-pitched yells. The defenders could have been anybody. At this distance it was impossible to identify a man.

Ben said: "How the hell do we play this? Charge in like the Goddam cavalry?"

Arch looked around. The timber to the north was nearer than that to the south. That would give them cover that would take them nearer to the attackers under fair cover. He turned his horse and got it on the move, spurring toward the trees. The animal was tired, but it tried for him. In a few minutes, they were stooping over their horses' necks under the trees, dodging this way and that around the trunks, heaving their rifles free.

The firing seemed to have risen to a crescendo now, but they could see little that was happening through the trees. But soon Arch rode into an open spot and turned right to the edge of timber. He halted and saw that he was as near as he could get to the fight.

As the others heaved up beside him, he put his rifle to his shoulder sighted on a buck broadside on to him and fired. The rider was flung clear as the horse somersaulted. The man landed full length, rolled, got to his feet and started to run. It took two more shots to drop him. By now the others were pouring shots into the attackers where it was safe to do so without hitting the attacked. For a few moments, the hard riding Indians seemed unaware that they were being shot at from another direction, but by the time two of their number had been cut down into the grass, they knew right enough.

One man halted his horse and stared blankly at Arch and the others, as if he were unable to believe his eyes. But when several shots hummed close, he kicked his horse into motion and rode off in the direction of the water. The paint pony didn't take a half-dozen jumps before lead, either from the defenders or from Arch's party, tore him from his saddle-pad and dumped him in the grass. The rest of the Indians were now in flight. Another died before they could get away. Arch tried to count them as they flew over the grass, beating at their racing ponies with bow-hafts and rifle butts. There were no more than five of them.

They stayed in the timber for a while, letting

the dust die, waiting for the sound of the Indians' retreat to die away.

"Now," Arch said, "we go in mighty easy. If they ain't our mules over yonder my name ain't Kelso. How many do you reckon is there, Ben?"

Ben squinted.

"I don't see no more'n two on their feet. Could be more lyin' down. Looks like some sort of earthwork they have there."

"All right. Let's go."

They walked their horses from the deep shadow of the trees, their rifles held across their knees, ready for instant action, knowing that if these were their raiders they were heading for men more deadly than the Apache.

They hadn't gone twenty yards when a shot was fired and sang close over their heads. They halted.

Charlie said: "That's what we wanted to know."

"How do we do it?" Ben asked.

"Mighty careful," Arch said. "We all come out of this alive. There's been enough men killed."

There was sudden movement from the defenders. A bulky figure heaved itself onto the back of a horse. The animal jumped forward, went over the low barricade and headed south toward the rocks and trees. Arch stood up in his stirrup-irons. He saw the heavily loaded mule following behind the horse and rider.

He shouted: "Pin the others down. That bastard's mine."

He raked his horse with iron and the animal jumped forward. He angled it around the east of the defenders and expected a shot at any moment, but none came. As he thundered by, a single man on one knee watched him go. He glanced back and saw that the others were trotting their horses forward. One of them threw up a gun and started firing. He faced front again and concentrated on the man he was after.

All he could see of him was a shape hunched forward in the saddle, but there was something familiar about it. He knew that he had seen the man before, which was probable if he came from Crewsville. The fellow's horse was tired and he was held back by the mule which was heavily laden, but Arch's horse was also tired and now with the sudden call to give all its speed, it was starting to flag. Arch fired a shot, not expecting to make a hit, but hoping that it might stop the man. It did not, however, and in seconds he was clattering through the rocks and heading into the trees. Arch tried to increase the pace, but the horse didn't have it to give. He reached timber about a hundred yards behind the pursued.

He was no sooner among the trees than a shot sounded and lead passed within inches of him. He swerved the horse to one side, sheltering behind the tree trunks and for a moment, so dark was it beneath the trees, that he could see nothing. There was, however, a sudden movement somewhere ahead of him and he glimpsed the man stepping into the saddle. Arch put his horse into motion, came into a clear space and saw that the mule and its line was tangled up in some brush. The man was cursing frantically and striving to free it. As Arch came nearer, the man turned in the saddle.

It was Doc Dooley.

In a flash everything settled into place. Arch should have known. The relentless execution of the attack on the wagons pointed to nobody else but Doc. The fact showed Arch that in the next few seconds he would not only have his hands full, but that he might not come out of this alive.

Doc made a quick movement with his right

hand and in the next few seconds he would not only have his hands saved Arch's life. Arch dropped away over the far side of his horse, dove under the animal, landed full stretch on the ground, had no time to sight the rifle and fired.

Doc's horse whirled wildly and ran into the mule. The rider came out of the saddle, whether by intent or accident Arch didn't know, but Doc was suddenly out of sight among the brush.

A shot came as Arch rolled. The bullet drove dirt up near his head and he continued the roll, dropping the rifle and heaving the Remington from leather. Doc's horse and mule reared and turned, smashing their way out of the brush, Arch caught sight of a shadowy shape and fired again. There was a crash of branches.

Did I kill him? Arch wondered.

He knew in a second. A shot. The lead plucked at his sleeve. Arch got his legs under him, reared to his feet and driving forward in one movement, charged. Doc fired twice, quickly and then Arch was into the brush and driving a shot into the man who appeared in front of him. Doc came in to him like a great bear, grabbing at him clumsily with both arms, making an animal growling noise deep in his throat. Arch gave way under the irresistible weight, hit the ground with his shoulders and hurled Doc free of the brush. Arch rolled and came to his feet.

Doc was on his hands and knees, face flecked with blood and dirt.

"Arch," he said, "let me go."

Arch was aware that he still had the Remington in his hand. He reckoned he had one shot left. He knew that his life depended on that one bullet.

"You killed Mel," he said.

That was enough for Doc. He knew that it was him or Arch. But he made another try.

"There's a hell of a lot of gold," he said. "Enough for us both."

Arch said coldly: "You have your gun, Doc. Try and use it."

A look of resignation came over the face of the man on the ground.

"It's empty," he said.

"Then leave it on the groond," Arch said, "and stand up. Move kind of slow."

Doc's reply was to throw himself flat, thrust the gun out on the end of a stiff arm and fire.

Arch took one step to the right, flicked up

the Remington and fired. A look of utter surprise came over Doc's face before it slammed down in the dirt. Arch stood very still for a moment, walked forward and rolled Doc over with a foot and saw that he had a hole through his right temple. For the first time in his life after killing a man, Arch knew no regret. He was trembling slightly and he wanted to sit down before his legs gave out on him, but he didn't. He drew air into his lungs in great gulps, reloaded the Remington and thrust it away. Then he turned and caught up the lines of the animals and walked out of the trees into the sunlight.

They came down wearily off the saddle, driving the loose mules, four very tired men. They sighted the wagons and saw that many figures moved among them. As they came nearer, they saw that there were as many soldiers as civilians there.

Ben laughed.

"Everybody's come," he said. "The law an' the army. Both a mite too late as usual."

They took their time about going down, there didn't seem to be anything to hurry for any more. But as they came closer to the wagons, driving the mules over the last ridge, Arch saw something to hurry for. A figure detached itself from the crowd and came running toward them. It was Martha. He urged his tired horse forward and met her halfway, swinging out of the saddle before the horse stopped and taking her in his arms.

Nothing could bring Mel back, nor the men who had died, but life was still good. Martha was crying gently and laughing at the same time. With his arm around her, he walked slowly toward the wagons. Men came forward to meet him.

THE END

Books by Matt Chisholm
in the Linford Western Library:

McALLISTER ON THE COMANCHE CROSSING
McALLISTER AND THE SPANISH GOLD
McALLISTER NEVER SURRENDERS
McALLISTER DIE-HARD
McALLISTER AND CHEYENNE DEATH
McALLISTER—QUARRY
McALLISTER FIRE-BRAND
THE TRAIL OF FEAR
RAGE OF McALLISTER
McALLISTER—WOLF-BAIT
A BULLET FOR BRODY
McALLISTER MAKES WAR
GUN LUST